IN THE SHADOWS

Lifepath Adventures: Mary Jones

RUTH KIRTLEY

© Ruth Kirtley 2009
First published 2009
ISBN 978 1 84427 374 4

Scripture Union
207–209 Queensway, Bletchley, Milton Keynes, MK2 2EB
Email: info@scriptureunion.org.uk
Website: www.scriptureunion.org.uk

Scripture Union Australia
Locked Bag 2, Central Coast Business Centre, NSW 2252
Website: www.scriptureunion.org.au

Scripture Union USA
PO Box 987, Valley Forge, PA 19482
Website: www.scriptureunion.org

Scripture quotations are taken from the Holy Bible, New International Version. Copyright © 1973, 1978, 1984 International Bible Society. Anglicisation copyright © 1979, 1984, 1989, 1995, 1996, 2001. Used by permission of Hodder and Stoughton Limited.

British Library Cataloguing-in-Publication Data
A catalogue record of this book is available from the British Library.

Printed and bound in India by Thompson Press India Limited

Cover design: Pink Habano
Internal layout: Author and Publisher Services

☙ Scripture Union is an international charity working with churches in more than 130 countries, providing resources to bring the good news of Jesus Christ to children, young people and families and to encourage them to develop spiritually through the Bible and prayer.

As well as our network of volunteers, staff and associates who run holidays, church-based events and school Christian groups, we produce a wide range of publications and support those who use our resources through training programmes.

My thanks to Marvin Baker and Sara Eade for their help and advice on the language and culture of the area where the story takes place, and for information on the life of Mary Jones

Bryn is a fictional character, but Mary Jones really existed. She was born in 1784 and lived in Llanfihangel-y-pennant. Her journey to Bala is part of her Lifepath Adventure!

Chapter One

Here comes the sun! It's floating out of the mist and warming me, up here on the Mountain. The night is over at last and I'm still alive! I'm wet and cold and I ache from lying on my bed of rock, but nothing happened. The mist is rolling away like smoke from a fire and I can see the track down to the valley below. Before I go, I want to look all ways and remember everything that I see. If I look carefully over the edge of this crag I can see, far below, the little lake that people say is bottomless. If I turn the other way I can see the great river, growing wider as it reaches the sea. I am so high! Up here I can see what the kites and buzzards see as they soar across the sky... and I'm so hungry I could eat Giant Idris for my breakfast!

She was right, of course, though there were times when I wasn't sure she would be. This was to be the big test, but she didn't make me do it. She'll most likely give me a proper telling off when she hears what I've done. But I wanted to do it. Wanted to prove to myself and all the others that what she says is true.

She's been so sure, all along the way. If she believes something she doesn't give up. Once she gets an idea in her head nothing stops her, and I should know! I can hardly believe the things I've done because of her... being up here, for example! I, Bryn, son of Madoc Parry the shepherd, have spent the night alone on the seat of Idris the Giant, in the territory of Gwyn the Hunter, and I've come to no harm.

All my life I've lived in the shadow of the Mountain. It looms above all the other mountains nearby and, believe me, we have many mountains here in Wales! I grew up knowing that it was a special mountain; a magical place with great power. It's a place to respect and also fear. In all weather and at all times of the year eyes are drawn to its steep slopes and rocky crags. On the days when the mist comes down and covers the top it's easy to believe that something secret is going on up here. For instance, maybe Giant Idris is tormenting some fool who has dared to climb up and sit between the three peaks that make his great chair. Or, on stormy nights when the wind howls, it can sound like Gwyn the Hunter is out rampaging with his great hounds, searching for some unfortunate soul to drag down to the Dark Place. Oh, there are lots of stories and many people believe them. And, even if they don't really believe them, those stories are useful. "Behave yourself, or the Giant will come down the Mountain for you!"

I was fearful like all the other children but, as well as fear, I could feel something pulling me up here. I would look up and think. What would it be like to climb, way up there? What would I be able to see from the top? What would happen to me? Well, now I know.

I must hurry down now, before the others start to wonder where I've gone. I must go carefully on the steep track. Mam says I'm more nimble than a mountain goat but the rocks are wet and it's easy to slip. I don't want to break my neck and be breakfast for the ravens!

1800 – a new century and a new adventure! I can't believe all that has happened to me in the past few years.

* * *

*W*e were both born here in the village, in the little valley in the mountains. Go down the wide valley with the long lake, through the big village and take the narrow track. This winds up and around the side of the hill. Keep the river beside you and you can't get lost. The hills close in and trees surround you for a while but, just around the corner, another valley opens out below. Go down, past the ruined castle on its high mound, and you're in our valley. Our village is small, with only a few families; grown-ups, children and some old people. We are all kinds; gentle and rough, clever and slow, some very strange, like Mad Bethan. We live in scattered cottages and farms. Everyone knows everyone, which can sometimes be a bit of a problem. There are more sheep than people here, that's for sure. They graze on the sides of the mountains and on the valley floor. They're everywhere!

Sometimes I think sheep are boring, stupid animals; not like Tegwyn and Bran, my Tada's dogs. But sheep are important to our village.

"Mr Rhys and his sheep keep our village alive," says my Tada. I think my father must be right because, without the sheep, Tada and the other shepherds would have no work. Without sheep there would be no wool for the women to spin into yarn, and without yarn there would be no work for the weavers. So those sheep keep most of us from going hungry.

I don't really remember noticing her until I was old enough to play with the other children, away from my own doorstep. Then I might see her in her garden or walking past our cottage with her mam. It wasn't long before I noticed that Mary, the daughter of Jacob Jones, was different. For one thing, she was cleaner than most of us. Even in winter when it's too cold to swim in the river and wash off the dust and the sheep muck that seems to stick to everything, Mary looked clean. Her face and hands looked as if she washed them every day! My sisters have so many tangles in their hair that they look like the manes of wild ponies, but Mary's hair is always neatly tied back. But there are six children in my family and Mary has no brothers or sisters, so I decided that it was easy for her mam to keep her clean and tidy.

But it wasn't just the being clean that made her different. She seemed to be so cheerful and I thought that was very strange because her tada was dead. Jacob Jones the weaver had died when she was little. In our village, everyone knows that if there's no man in the home to bring in the money life is very, very hard. Neighbours will try to help but we're all poor. People have little enough for themselves and there's rarely much left over for others. Mary and her mam were on their own, trying to do the weaving as well as all the women's work. By the time I began to notice Mary she was already learning to thread and work the loom with her mam. The two of them were hard at it all day long; her mam on the loom and Mary cleaning, cooking, looking after the hens and bees. Work, work, work. Mam would shake her head and say, "How does the poor woman manage?"

Of course, all we children have our jobs to do. As soon as we're old enough we start to help our families. My first jobs were collecting firewood and then digging the vegetable patch and fetching the water to the cottage for Mam. Now Gwenna and little Luc often help with those things and I have other jobs. I sometimes work with Tada and my older brother Huw, out with the sheep. I like being with the men and the dogs but I don't like those other jobs. The water bucket is heavy and slops all down my leg when I hurry. Digging is the most boring thing in the world! I do my jobs as fast as I can and then I run off quick to the river in case Mam thinks of something else

I can do. If she catches me I moan and make a big fuss, but when Tada calls me I go willingly.

Even though she and her mam were so poor and had to work so hard I never heard Mary grumble. Even when she had to do a really messy, boring job like picking the twigs and muck out of the fleeces before they were washed. I would run past her cottage, on my way to join the other boys at the river or the ruined castle, and I would see her. She'd be sitting on her doorstep with a stinky fleece in her lap, humming away to herself. She could hardly ever go out and play like the rest of us but she would call "Good day!" as I passed her door. Sometimes she'd stop for a while, on her way to do an errand, and she'd join in the game we were playing. But then she'd say "Must be going now," and off she'd hurry.

The first time I remember speaking to Mary properly was one day when we met by the river. I remember because it was also the day I began to understand why she and her mam were different. I'd been fishing with some of the boys and my line had got tangled in a bush on the riverbank. The others had got tired of waiting and gone off home, leaving me pulling and muttering. I got it free at last and then I slipped on a wet rock and cut my big toe. Mary came along the track from the big village and there I was, limping home and leaving red dots of blood in the dust behind me.

"Good day to you, Bryn Parry," said she. "What have you done to your foot?"

"It's just a cut," I said, trying to limp faster, as if it was nothing to bother about.

"I have something that will help," she said.

"Don't trouble yourself!" I was wishing she would go away because I was feeling very foolish.

She shrugged and walked past me down the track and then she turned round.

"If you keep walking as slow as that you'll miss your supper, though you may be in time for breakfast tomorrow!" She was grinning at me, as if it was a big joke.

"Humph!"

"It must be very sore."

Well, she was right about that! My toe had started to throb as if someone was hitting it with a hammer. So I stopped and she put down her basket. First she made me put my foot back in the river and wash the blood and dust off. Then she took out the cleanest handkerchief I'd ever seen and dried my foot. After that she reached into her basket, took out a jar and stuck a finger into it. Then she spread some sticky stuff on to the cut.

"Yowch!" I yelled. She laughed at me, sitting there holding my foot and making faces.

"You'll live, Bryn Parry. Stop making a fuss; that's good honey I put on your cut. Our bees worked hard to make it."

"Honey?" I was amazed because honey is a rare treat in our family. My mam has enough to do without keeping bees as well, though there are people in the village who do. "We put honey on our bread, not on our feet!"

"Well, it will keep your cut clean and help it to heal fast," she replied, as she quickly tied the handkerchief round my foot and knotted it neatly. "There, now we can be home before supper."

We walked back to the village together and I realised that already my toe wasn't throbbing as badly.

"What have you done to yourself this time?" asked Mam when I got home. As I explained, she gasped and a look of horror came over her face.

"What were you thinking of, letting that girl put things on your foot? Wash it off! Wash it off quickly!"

"Aw Mam, it's only honey and it made my toe feel better!"

"Honey indeed! Listen to me my boy; you wash it off this very minute!"

Mam pushed me on to a stool, pulled off the handkerchief and threw it on the fire. Then she looked hard at my toe, tutting and frowning.

"What's the matter?" Ceris, my big sister was standing in the doorway.

"Watch the baby while I deal with your stupid brother!" Mam ordered her as she dragged me outside and poured a jug of water over my foot. I hopped about, shouting, "Stop, Mam! It's only honey! Where's the harm in that?"

Then Mam stopped and looked at me sternly.

"You must be careful of that girl and her family. They and their friends are not like the rest of us. They've changed. They've left the old ways that have suited us and our fathers and our fathers' fathers before them."

"But... " I didn't understand what she was saying but she wouldn't let me speak.

"They've started to follow strange new teachings that Outsiders have brought to the valley. They don't go to the church with the rest of us now. They go off and meet with others of their kind; creeping about in the dark and getting up to no good! They're no better than Mad Bethan!" She filled the water jug again and handed it to me.

"You scrub that foot and clean off every scrap of that potion. Goodness knows what bad magic she's put into you!"

Chapter Two

*M*agic? I couldn't see how a bit of honey on a sore foot could be bad magic. After that I began to watch Mary and her mam. I wanted to see what made Mam say those things about them. I looked carefully at my big toe every morning and it seemed just the same. It didn't swell up or fall off and the cut healed cleanly. Surely that was a good thing? There's plenty of talk about magic around here. Hens not laying, things going missing, people with the bellyache; it's often blamed on magic. People mutter and wonder who's making mischief and usually Mad Bethan gets the blame.

She's old and bent, with no teeth and a face all bumpy and crinkled like one of last year's potatoes. Her clothes are ragged and patched and she looks very strange. She takes long walks around the fields and hills, muttering to herself and collecting plants and berries in a basket. Some people say she uses them to make spells but that seems to be a waste of good food when she's likely as hungry as the rest of us. She lives in a cottage that stands alone, outside the village and we're not supposed to go near. I know some of the older girls sneak there at night sometimes. Ceris and her friends went, asking Bethan to make them love potions. I heard them whispering about it but I don't know if she made them anything. If she really does spells I don't think that it's powerful bad magic.

Mary and her mam didn't look like Mad Bethan and the only things I saw them collecting in their baskets were things for the cooking pot, just like the rest of us. So what else was it that made people say they were up to no good? Well, I soon realised Mam was right about one thing; they didn't go to the church any more.

Sunday mornings Mam makes us wash our face and hands and tries to tidy our hair. You can hear Ceris and Gwenna yowling as she tugs the comb through the tangles. I keep well away and just wet my hair and smooth it down like the men do. Then Mam ties on her best shawl and puts on her hat. As soon as we hear the "ting-ting-ting" from the bell, we all hurry down to the church. It sits in its little round yard, with a high stone wall around it to keep the sheep out. We shuffle through the door and the men pull off their caps. Then we squeeze into our pews and sit and stand and sing and pray and listen to the Reverend talking, talking, talking. He sounds like an old sheep, going "Baa-baa... Go-o-o-d... baa-baa... si-i-i-n... baa-baa... he-e-e-ll... baa-baa"! Winter's all right because we're all cosied together and it's nice and warm but, in the summer it's dreadful to be stuck inside when the sun's shining.

"Why do we have to go to church?" I asked Tada one Sunday, long ago.

"Because we must," he told me.

"But why? It's so boring!"

"Boring it may be," he replied as he tied on a clean neckerchief, "But Mr Rhys expects it, so that's that."

I looked when we got to church that Sunday and, sure enough, there was Mr Rhys and his family, sitting at the front. He manages the farms for the man who owns all the land hereabouts. Every so often he'd turn and look around the church, to see who was there. He'd catch the eye of one of the men and nod. If one of us children fidgeted or made a sound he would turn and frown at us. Then he'd turn back to the Reverend, looking as if he'd never heard anything so interesting in his life before!

"What would happen if you didn't go to church, Tada?" I asked as we walked home again.

"I'm not going to risk finding out," he replied.

"But what's church for?

Tada looked annoyed. "Stop your questions, boy! We go because we must. We don't need to understand what it's for. Where's the harm in spending an hour there each week, even if it's all moonshine? If it keeps Mr Rhys happy, I keep my job. I go to church and while you live under my roof so will you!"

So, week after week, we go to the church, but I don't understand why Mr Rhys goes and why he thinks we should go, too. Anyway, one day I decided I'd ask Mary why she and her mam didn't go to the church any more. I made sure Mam didn't see me go to her cottage because I didn't want any trouble.

Mary and her mam live in a cottage beside the river, just by the packhorse bridge. It is a damp spot, with not much space for a garden. They have to use some land further along the road to grow their vegetables and flowers. The track that goes over the mountains to the market town in the next valley passes right by their front door. As I came near I could hear the "click-thunk, clack-thunk" of the loom, coming from inside the cottage. I knew that meant her mam was in there weaving, but I needed to find Mary. I was worried that I might have to knock at the door and speak to her mam but then I saw her. She was over in their vegetable patch, digging potato plants out of the ground. I hadn't spoken to Mary since she mended my toe and I felt a bit awkward.

"Good day to you, Bryn Parry," she said with a smile. "Your toe is healed?" I shuffled my feet in the dust and nodded.

"Good as new, thank you."

She smiled again and picked up the stalks of a potato plant, to shake the soil off. Then she started to pull the potatoes off. Now I must speak or she would think me very strange.

"Er, I have a question for you." That wasn't what I meant to say but, never mind; I had started and now I must go on. "I want to know why you don't go to the church with the rest of us," I said, all in a rush. "I want to know why you've changed."

Mary stopped, wiped her hands on her apron and looked at me.

"We follow a new path," she replied. "A way that has led many people to know God better."

"My Mam says that Outsiders have brought the new teaching into our village," I said. Mary nodded.

"It's true; the teaching has come from far away, beyond our mountains and Societies of believers are starting in many places. We have joined the Society in the big village. It's like a church. We meet there to hear what God has to teach us and how we may follow his path more closely."

"But there's a church here. The Reverend talks about God; why don't you go and listen to him?"

Mary bent to pick up the digging fork and the basket of potatoes. "Before we learned of the new path it was hard to know God. The path wasn't clear and God was far away. He was like the Mountain when its top is covered in mist and you can only see tiny bits as the clouds move across."

I took the basket from her and we started to walk back to her cottage.

"How can you know God?" I wanted to know. "God lives in church and only the Reverend and Mr Rhys are interested."

"We have learned that you can know God!" said Mary and she looked excited. "God made us and he loves us. He wants us to follow his path and he speaks to us."

"Speaks to you?" I almost dropped the basket. "What does he sound like?" I laughed, thinking of the Reverend. I spoke in his old sheep voice. "Ma-a-a-ry, Ma-a-a-ry, this is Go-o-o-d speaking!" Mary's cheeks went very pink and she glared at me.

"I am trying to answer your questions, Bryn Parry. If you will not be serious then you can give me back that basket and go and stick your head in the river!"

I was sorry that I'd upset her. "Please explain; I'm listening, really I am."

We had reached her cottage and she took the basket. Then she began to take the potatoes and wash the dirt from them. She handed me a knife.

"Here, make yourself useful!" Then she passed me the washed potatoes to cut in pieces and put in a pot by the door. Women's work! But somehow I didn't dare refuse and, anyway, I wanted to know more.

"God doesn't speak in a voice," she explained patiently. "We hear him speak through his Word; that's what we call the Bible."

"The Bible? You mean that great, black book that the Reverend reads out of in the church?"

"Yes, but oh how different it sounds when someone like William Huw reads to us!" Mary's busy hands stopped and she looked at me with smiling eyes. "He's been a follower of God's path for many years and he loves the Bible. He's read and studied it from one end to the other. When he speaks and explains the Bible it's as though we can hear God speaking to us. I've learned more about God since we joined the Society than we ever did at church!"

"Where do you go to hear God speaking?" I wanted to know. Mary picked up another potato.

"We meet in an evening or on Sundays, in the homes of other members of the Society," she said. "We travel over the hill to the big village, or sometimes further still. Children do not usually join the Society or go to the meetings. I started to go with Mam when my Tada died. She had no one to carry the lantern and walk with her when the path was dark. I have done this for many years now. At first I found it hard to understand what the men who spoke were saying. Now I've been listening for so long that some of it has started to make sense."

"What do they say, these men who speak?"

"Well, the Bible seems to be full of different things. Sometimes they read stories to us about people long ago who followed God's path, or they read parts that are letters, written to the people who were followers. They explain about Jesus, who was sent by God to lead us back to him. From the Bible they teach us how everything fits together, to show how God loves us and has a plan for the world he made. Some of it is difficult but some is exciting!"

"Do you have to sit still and listen, like we do in church?"

"Of course! And sometimes the meeting is so long that people go to sleep for a while," Mary laughed. "But no one minds because we all work hard and some have walked a long way to get there and they're very tired when they arrive."

I sometimes saw heads nodding and eyes closing in church on Sundays. The Reverend would frown and someone would quickly nudge the sleepy person awake again. Heads might nod but no one would dare to snore in church!

"But don't you fear Mr Rhys? It's dangerous to stay away from church; my Tada says so."

Mary frowned. "Mr Rhys, Idris or Gwyn of the Mountain; they're all the same. They hold no fear for us now."

"Be careful what you say!" I warned, looking behind her to where the Mountain towered. "Remember when old Gethin drove his sheep too high up the Mountain for the summer grazing? People said he was a fool; that

They wouldn't like it. He just laughed but then he lost five of his best ewes in a landslide."

"Accidents happen," she replied.

"Well, maybe they do but Mr Rhys has real power. If we want to eat we need the work that he gives."

Mary nodded. "I know, but he doesn't give us our work. Mam can sell what we weave to the fulling mill near the big village. We are safe enough, though there are others who are being brave. Eli Owen and Morgan Preece from the big village, they both work for Mr Rhys and now they have joined the Society, too. It may be hard for them, but God promises to protect his followers when they are in trouble. He provides all we need."

I looked at her worn-out clothes and the pot with nothing but potatoes in it and I thought about the bit of bacon Tada brought home last night. Today we would eat meat and, when the carrier's cart came through the village, Mam might sometimes get us a treat like fish from the town by the sea. Tada had a job and we had a little money. It seemed to make sense to me to keep Mr Rhys happy and not go off following this new path that Mary talked about, however exciting she seemed to think it was.

Chapter Three

 $\mathcal{I}$ didn't speak to Mary again for a while, though I saw her around the village sometimes. She would smile or say "Good day", and if I was alone and I was sure Mam wasn't looking, I would nod to show I'd seen her. But I was pulled two ways. Part of me thought that she and the others like her were dangerous; doing strange things and asking for trouble. I needed to keep far away from them just as Mam said. But I was curious, too. I wanted to find out how someone who was only a girl could be so fearless. Her courage was not play-acting, I could see. She really didn't seem to be afraid of Them, up there on the Mountain or of powerful Mr Rhys. So I kept my eyes and ears open, which I've always found is a useful thing to do.

My ears heard the whispers between the womenfolk as Mary or her mam passed through the village. Even if I couldn't hear what was said the frown or shake of the head and the "Tsk, tsk" were clear enough. My eyes caught the sign to ward off evil that some made behind their backs, as they did when Mad Bethan passed.

One night I heard Tada and Huw, arriving home from the fields, talking to the other shepherds as they passed our cottage.

"Eli Owen is a fool! I heard him with my own ears. 'No sir,' says he, to Mr Rhys. 'I will not leave the path I've chosen.' Stood there and said it to his face!"

"The man must have taken too much sun; it's turned his brain!"

"No, he was as sane as you and I but he wouldn't change his mind."

"But what did Mr Rhys say to that?"

"He was not pleased! 'Well, if I don't see you in the church this Sunday coming, then I don't want to see you ever again. If you won't worship with the rest of my men then you shan't work with them either!'"

"The man's mad! What does he think he's going to feed his wife and all those children on?"

"Huh, 'The good Lord will provide,' says he."

"Fine words, but they won't fill empty bellies..."

The speakers moved on and I remembered what Mary had said about others being brave. So she was telling the truth; there really were others who were following this new path. Then a few nights later, I was out feeding scraps to the pig and I saw the light of a lantern, bobbing through the darkness. Two figures, wrapped in shawls, were hurrying along the track to the big village. I knew it was Mary and her mam, off to one of their mysterious meetings. Who would want to walk into the darkness for miles and miles, at the end of a long day, when normal folk were thinking of their beds? I had more questions for Mary, but they had to wait.

It was late spring and I was busy, helping Tada and the other men with the shearing of the sheep. I was too young to do the shearing itself; it takes a man's strength to hold down the sheep and a broad hand to clip off their wool with the big, sharp-bladed shears. But I was anxious to prove how useful I could be and to show Tada that I was almost a man.

I love to watch Bran and Tegwyn circle round the sheep and bring them across the fields to the shearing pens. I think they can run faster than a stone flying from my slingshot. I hope one day I'll have a dog that I can train to come and go to my whistle.

Helping at the shearing is hard work. I have to stand by the pen's opening and make sure all those stupid sheep go through and don't suddenly bolt off again for no reason. Then I must pull the hurdle across to close the gap and wait to take the shorn sheep from the shearer and guide them into the other pen. They always look so funny without their shaggy grey winter coats; running about and baaing in their Reverend voices! Next I have to collect the fleeces and fold them neatly so that they're easier to carry. Fleeces are very heavy and very dirty and by the end of the day my arms ache and I smell like a sheep, though my hands are soft from the oil in the wool.

Mam won't let us in the cottage until we've been to the river to wash, so off I ran to our favourite pool. Tada and the others were driving the sheep back out to the pasture so I could enjoy the water while it was clean and clear, before they came and churned up the mud and pebbles. I put my head under the water to cool my face and practise blowing bubbles. I could stay under the water longer than any of the other boys and this was something I was very proud of when I was younger.

Well, what with the water in my ears and eyes, at first I didn't notice Mary when I stood up again. But there she was, standing on the bank, watching me.

"So, it's you, Bryn Parry," said she. "I feared someone was drowning and wondered should I get myself wet to save them!"

I could see she was laughing and not at all worried.

"I don't need your help, Mary Jones." I was wondering how foolish I had looked and I was annoyed that she had seen me.

"I can see that now," she replied. "You swim as well as any fish; I think you are very clever."

That made me feel better and I waded out of the water to join her. She was carrying her basket, though today it was empty.

She saw me looking at her empty basket. "We've just come back from the big village," she said. "Today we sold all our eggs and honey. Mam has bought a piece of mutton and I am looking for sorrel, though I know it's late in the day and others will have been looking earlier."

She didn't seem to mind that she would likely have a wasted journey. I thought at first she was just excited about the thought of a good meal but I found out it was something else that had put that big smile on her face.

"Have you heard the news, Bryn Parry?" What news could that be? Had someone's cow fallen down a well? Had Padrig's tada got drunk again and been seeing fairies? Or were the French invading Fishguard again? Mary looked mighty pleased about something. I shrugged and waited for her to tell me.

"A school is opening in the big village!" She seemed very excited at this news, though I couldn't see why. If someone had found a crock of gold and was going to share it with us, now that would be exciting!

Mary seemed disappointed that I wasn't jumping and turning cartwheels at her news.

"Don't you understand?" she said, "We're to have a school! We can go there and learn to read and write. A man called Mr Ellis is coming; I heard about it at the Society meeting. People are so glad. He'll come and teach us our letters and then we'll be able to read!"

Well, I still couldn't see what all the fuss was about but she seemed so happy she was almost dancing. I was going to say something else but then I saw the men coming down to the river so I turned away quickly and hurried home.

* * *

*N*ot long after that the news was buzzing round the village like a swarm of bees. Some were not sure but most people seemed to think it was a good idea.

"Just think!" said Mam to us children. "How wonderful to have people in the family who can read. When you can read, you'll be as good as Mr Rhys or the Reverend! You'll be able to get a fine job and make lots of money!"

"Huh, reading's not for the likes of us," said Tada. "A strong body and skill with the sheep is more important than spending all day chanting letters. Mr Rhys may be able to read and reckon but he needs us men to do the real work."

I still wasn't sure that school would be exciting. I like to be outdoors. Climbing the hills, looking for a buzzard's nest, chasing rabbits with Bran and Tegwyn, watching the storm clouds swoop over the Mountain and hearing the thunder crack: that's exciting. Mam won, though and I was sent to the school, along with Luc. Gwenna was too little and she stayed with Mam and the baby and Ceris stayed to help her. Tada needed Huw to help with the sheep.

The first day there was a crowd of us children walking the track to the big village, each of us carrying our bread and cheese for later. Mary was there, looking clean and tidy, and hurrying along as if she was afraid to waste any time. It was a bright, sunny day; just the weather for fishing but I was willing to give school a try.

The school was held in the church hall. The big village has a much bigger church than ours and a hall beside it. We waited outside till a man in a suit came out and called us all together. His boots were shiny and he spoke like a gentleman.

"My name is Mr Ellis, and I am the master of the circulating school which will meet here for the next few months. If you are willing to work hard and pay attention you will learn much. I am very glad to be here but you need to know that I will not tolerate bad behaviour, foul language or laziness. My time is precious and there are other villages who need a school, so do not think I will stay here long if I decide it is not worth my while!"

Hm, stern words, but I could see a smile at the corner of his mouth. We all lined up and marched inside, girls sitting on one side of the room and boys on the other. The benches were long and shiny, like in church, but the room looked very different. On the walls were many pictures and lengths of paper, covered in strange marks. Behind where Mr Ellis stood was a big blackboard, standing on legs. On it were more marks in white; I had no idea what they meant but I was interested to find out.

First, Mr Ellis said a prayer and then we all had to tell him our names and where we lived. There were many children there, from both villages and from along the valley, too. It took a long time and some people were scared to speak out in front of everyone. Luc wet himself but then he does that quite often. I was proud to say that I was Bryn, son of Madoc Parry the shepherd and I looked Mr Ellis in the eye.

Later we started to listen to and repeat the names of the marks he pointed to on the black board. At first the sounds were strange in my mouth: "Ay – Bee – See" but slowly I began to recognise some of the shapes when he pointed at them, though I doubted I'd ever remember all of them.

It was good to go outside at midday. We were able to eat and run about for a while in the sunshine. I saw Mary and some of the girls sitting on the ground, drawing some of the shapes we had been learning in the dust with sticks. After our break we went back to work, listening and repeating and then Mr Ellis took a white stick and made long strings of shapes on the black board. Of course I know now that they were words but it was a marvel to see him writing so fast and neat.

"Now, children, we will all learn this verse," he said. "It is important and to remember it will be valuable for you. Repeat after me, 'Your word is a lamp to my feet and a light to my path'. Are you ready?"

We muttered and mumbled our way through with just a few clear voices; mostly from the girls. Mr Ellis made us repeat it many times until he was satisfied that we had learned it.

"That verse can be found in the Bible," he told us. "Psalm one hundred and nineteen and verse one hundred and five. Tomorrow I want to see how many of you can repeat it to me, from memory."

I looked over to where Mary was sitting. Her lips were moving and I was sure she was already repeating the verse to herself. What was it she'd said about the Bible? Wasn't it something about God speaking from it and it being his word? Now we had been told that the word was a lamp! I was very confused and my head was full of all those white marks and strange sounds like "Ay – Bee – See... " When Mr Ellis announced that school was over for the day I was the first out of the door and I didn't stop running until I could see the roofs of our village and the smell of Mam's baking came to meet me!

Chapter Four

By the end of the first week I had decided that school was not for me. True, I could now chant "Ay – Bee – See" right through to "Ex – Wye – Zed", but putting together all the sounds these letters made in order to read words was beyond me. Also, the weather stayed warm and the sunshine was inviting. Some of my friends had already stopped coming and I could see them down in the river as I trudged to school in the morning. I hoped that Tada might need me but, no, he had decided that Mam was right and that I must go and learn to read. Besides, they seemed to think that someone should take Luc, to make sure he didn't fall in the river or get eaten by wolves on the way to school!

"You go to that school, son and one day you'll be a fine gentleman with your reading and writing," said Mam.

"Huh, more likely I'll go blind with wearing out my eyes on all those letters. I tell you, Mam, it's killing me!" I said.

"Nonsense!" she laughed. "This is a wonderful chance for you. You'll go to school and that's that. Now, off you go, shoo!" and she hurried me out of the cottage with her broom, like I was one of her hens.

To makes things worse, Mary and a few others were really enjoying themselves at school. On the second morning, when Mr Ellis asked had anyone memorised the verse from the day before, some hands went up and some children tried to repeat it. One or two could only remember the first bit but some could say the whole thing. Then Mary bounced out of her seat and she repeated it perfectly. She had also remembered where it was found in the Bible. Then she said the whole of the ABC and, when Mr Ellis gave her the white stick, she wrote some of the letters on the board!

Mr Ellis praised everyone who tried; especially the little ones, because it was harder for them. But you could see that he was very surprised at what Mary had done. As the week went on it was clear that some children were learning much faster than the rest of us. While we were still plodding through the ABC they were starting to read and write whole words. Mr Ellis had some slates that they could use, to practice making their own marks. Soon they were sitting together, on one side of the room, their pencils squeak-squeaking as they copied what he had written on the board. Mary was there, of course, and I could see her with her head bent, scribbling away, or leaning over to help someone else. Whatever Mr Ellis asked us to memorise she did it.

I must confess that I didn't learn any of the verses that Mr Ellis set us. I tried at the start but they just wouldn't stick and there were always more exciting things to do after school finished. As I've already said, I had decided that school was not for me. But, no matter what I said, Mam had decided it was, so I had to keep going.

You'd think that if someone was as clever as Mary they would enjoy showing off but it was as if she hadn't noticed how much better than the rest of us she was. In the schoolroom she didn't look around; she kept her eyes fixed on Mr Ellis or on what he wrote on the board. It was almost as if she had forgotten that the rest of us were there.

Outside at break-time, though, Mary still spent time with some of the other girls; practising their letters in the dust or playing girls' games. Some children wouldn't play with her, but even though many parents thought she and her mam were strange or even dangerous, we children made up our own minds. Yes, she was clever and sometimes she said strange things but she was harmless.

One day I came across a group of girls and little children, sitting quietly in a corner of the yard, all listening to Mary. I edged closer to try and hear what she was saying.

"...and Goliath the giant said to David, 'Am I a dog that you come after me with a stick!' and he cursed David. But David answered, 'You come at me with sword and spear and battleaxe but I come at you in the name of the Lord Almighty!'" I could see Luc sitting there with his thumb in his mouth, eyes big and round.

"What happened? Did the giant kill David?" asked one of the girls.

"Oh, no!" Mary laughed. "Remember, he had the Lord Almighty to help him. As Goliath moved closer to attack him, David put a stone in his slingshot and shot him there, bang! right in the middle of his forehead!" she pointed at her head and Luc bounced up and down, shouting "Got 'im, got 'im!"

"The story isn't finished yet," said Mary. "David ran over to Goliath, pulled out the giant's sword and cut off his head, ker-runch!" The girls shuddered and pulled faces but Luc jumped up and started waving an imaginary sword around his head. One of the girls pulled him back down on to the ground and shushed him. "Let Mary finish the story!"

"Well," said Mary. "Then the enemy army ran and God's people chased them far away. So God's people were saved; all because David believed that God would help him."

"What happened to David next?" someone asked. Mary shrugged.

"I don't know. I haven't heard the next part of the story yet but I'll tell you when I do."

I thought that sounded a mighty fine story and I would tell it to Huw when he got home, only I had missed the first part. So on the walk home from school that day, I asked Mary to tell me the whole story again and she was happy to do that.

"Where did you learn such a good story?" I asked. "It's better than the ones Mam tells, of Gwyn and Idris."

She stopped and looked at me very seriously. "But this story isn't like the foolish old ones we hear, about giants and evil ghosts. This story is true!"

I looked up at the Mountain as she said that. Today it looked beautiful; all browns and greys against the clear, blue sky. Today it almost looked friendly but I know how quickly it can change. When the clouds cover the summit and the sky turns grey as slate I feel sure that Someone is watching us, maybe even hearing what we say.

"Be careful what you say, Mary Jones!" I warned her. "Those stories are very old and they must be true if the grown-ups believe them. If their stories are not true then neither is yours!"

Mary tossed her head and looked determined. "My story is true. It really happened; the preacher at the Society meeting told us."

"So where did he hear the story?"

"From the Bible, of course!"

* * *

I thought about that and wondered were there any other stories like that one in the Bible? I like stories about battles and giants and warrior kings doing great deeds with lots of sword-fighting and blood. I don't think we ever heard anything as exciting as that story from the Reverend! If the Bible held exciting stories, maybe that was why Mary thought it was so special? I waited for a chance to speak to her again and I soon got it. One day, after school, I was up on the hill behind the village.

I had climbed into a tree near the track where I thought I had seen a buzzard's nest. I climbed as high as I dared but I couldn't see a nest so I was coming down again when I saw Mary, walking quickly up the track and carrying her basket as usual. I waited until she was right under the tree and then I dropped on to the track in front of her. My, did she scream!

"Bryn Parry, you deserve to break your stupid neck!" she shouted. I just grinned and picked up her basket while she recovered.

"So where are you off to in such a hurry?"

"Huh, you half-kill me from fright and now you want to know my business?"

"Well, it isn't time for school, so why are you hurrying?"

Mary sighed and then smiled. "If you promise never to jump out at me again, I'll tell you."

"I promise," I said. "I swear by the great giant Idris... "

Mary waved her hand impatiently. "Oh, stop that nonsense and listen; I haven't time to waste. I'm going to Pendry's farm, if you must know. I'm taking some mending that I've done for Mrs Pendry."

"You don't need to hurry," I said. "Why walk so fast all that way? It's such a hot day."

"If I am quick I will have time to read their Bible."

"They have a Bible?" I was surprised at that, as no one I know has any books, though I suppose someone like Mr Rhys might have some; he's rich enough.

"They do," said Mary. "It's the only one hereabouts, apart from the one in the church, of course. Now that I'm able to read a bit I want to practise and I specially want to be able to read more of the Bible. At the Society meetings the preacher decides what to read and I can see there is so much more in there that I haven't heard yet!"

"Mrs Pendry lets you go into her house to read the Bible?" I had seen Mrs Pendry and I thought she was quite grand.

Mary nodded. "Yes, she's very kind. I do jobs for her, and every week she lets me go right into the parlour, to read their Bible. It lies on a special table and it's covered with a cloth. The first time I went she spoke very sternly. She wanted to be sure that I was gentle and would turn the pages carefully. Now, all I have to do is show my hands, so she can be sure they're clean. And if I'm wearing my clogs, I leave them outside, so as not to dirty her floors."

"You go every week?" I was amazed. She seemed to think that this was a wonderful thing but I thought it sounded like more school to me. Fancy wanting to read even when it wasn't a school day!

"Yes! And now I know lots more from the Bible; not just stories about God's long-ago people and the Psalms and letters that they wrote, but more about Jesus. God sent him to us to show us how to live godly lives."

Her eyes shone while she spoke and I could see that she was very excited. All because of a book!

Mary turned and set off up the track again. "You've kept me talking long enough, Bryn Parry! Goodbye."

Then I remembered why I'd wanted to talk to her.

"Find another story like that one about the giant!" I shouted after her.

* * *

The weeks passed and I kept going to school most days. Sometimes Mam would need me to do something for her and I was more glad to help her than I ever used to be. Also I was hoping that, once the summer began, I would go with the men when they took the sheep up to the high pastures. We would live up at the hafod on the mountains and I'd be too far away to go to the school then! After I had helped Mam I would try and find a reason to stay home, but she wouldn't budge.

"No, son, you go there and you learn all you can. I hear that Glynis and Trefor Morris can read many words now and write their own name; their mother never stops telling me."

"Huh, that Trefor is just like a girl. He won't join in the fights and he can't even throw a stone straight!"

Mam took no notice. "And everyone is talking of Mary Jones, too. Her mother may keep strange company but that girl knows how to work hard and they say she only needs to hear a thing once and she remembers it. Now why can't you be like those children? Our family needs someone who can read!"

Well, I didn't want to learn to read and write and I didn't want to be like those goody-goody Morrises. I wished they lived in another village so we didn't have to keep hearing how well they were doing. I even began to get annoyed with Mary. It was clear that she was cleverer than most of us but it was also true that she worked harder, too. It must have been very hard for her mam to manage without Mary to help her and I know that some days, when there was too much work for her to do alone, Mary had to stay home from school. Even so, she still managed to learn more than everyone else and remember it, too! So what with Mam wanting me to be like the clever children and me seeing Mary working so hard but seeming to enjoy it, I felt very discouraged. Never, ever would I be as good as that. I went to school but now I began planning how I could stay away for ever!

Chapter Five

Mr Ellis was a very patient man. He didn't seem to want to give up on any of us; even the knuckle-heads like me! Day after day he repeated the lessons to us, going over and over what he had said the day before and the weeks before that. Some of the work was not hard. If I'd had a mind to, I could probably have learned it, for I believe I'm not stupid. I think maybe Mr Ellis knew this and that's why he kept on. The trouble was that I had no interest in learning. I had decided that I would not learn and nothing would change me.

More and more of the other children moved to the side of the room with Mary and got the slates to use. Soon there were only a few left on my side. There were some younger children like Luc, Daft Garod, who thinks he's a bird most of the time, and me. It was time for me to move: not across the room but out of it!

I began to come late to school and then I tried to annoy Mr Ellis in different ways. I would give stupid answers to his questions or, when his back was turned, I'd pull some girl's hair or flick the ear of a boy nearby. They would fuss and complain, and I would look innocent. One day I found a nice, fresh cow-pat near the school. I tramped my feet in it until they were well covered and then made sure I walked around the schoolroom a lot before I sat down.

"Urgh! Mr Ellis, sir! Bryn Parry has made a dreadful stink. Look at his feet!"

Mr Ellis sighed, came over to where I sat and looked down at me.

"Well, Master Parry, I think it's time we parted company, don't you? It's plain to me that you have a quick and clever brain, but for some reason you don't wish to use it for anything sensible. I'm sad and disappointed, but I must now ask you to take your disgusting-smelling feet out of my school and kindly not return. Good day to you!"

I jumped to my feet and made for the door, waving to the others as I left. I saw Mary looking in my direction. She rolled her eyes and shook her head at me and then turned back to her slate. I ran out of the room and straight to the river to wash my feet. Then I went up to the castle and found some of the other boys who didn't go to school. We had a fine time throwing stones at the jackdaws and being brave knights, fighting off the English.

When the sun told me it would be break-time I went back to the school and peered through the railings, to see if Mary was telling stories in the yard. There she was, with a group around her, but they were too far away for me to hear. For a moment I wondered if my plan had been such a good one but then I remembered that the whole day was mine and away I ran.

* * *

*M*am gave me a good telling-off when she found out that Mr Ellis had sent me home.

"I think I must just be too stupid," I lied. "Mr Ellis has so many children to teach; he hasn't time to waste on the likes of me." I tried to look sad but that was hard. Mam looked at me with narrow eyes but I stared back without blinking and she said no more. She then gave me a lot of jobs to do, but I didn't mind because I would be outside in the sunshine, not sitting on that hard bench any more.

Later in the day I saw the children coming home from school. I went to meet them because I had to make sure that Luc didn't tell Mam what had really happened. It was easy enough to persuade him to keep quiet if I let him use my slingshot for a day in payment. Then I saw Mary hurrying home, alone. I could see her mouth moving and, as she came nearer, I could hear her.

"I lift up my eyes to the hills - where does my help come from? My help comes from the Lord, the Maker of earth - no, that's wrong - the Maker of heaven and earth."

She saw me and stopped. "I hope you are proud of yourself, Bryn Parry. God has given you a brain and you won't use it. Don't you understand how lucky we are to have a school and a teacher like Mr Ellis? There are so many villages where there is no school and soon Mr Ellis will have to move on to one of them. We need to take our chance while we can and you've wasted yours!"

I was surprised at her anger and so I laughed and changed the subject. "Got any more of those stories? I would really like to hear one."

"I'm sorry," said she, looking at me sternly. "I have work to do. You may have time to waste, but I don't!" She marched off, with her feet kicking up little puffs of dust behind her.

* * *

After that I would go looking for Mary and try to get her to tell me more stories. This wasn't easy because she was at school or working at home and Mam kept me busy, too. Sometimes Luc came home from school and tried to tell me the latest one that Mary had told them. He would forget bits and muddle the story till it made no sense at all. When I met Mary about the village or near her cottage she would smile, but when I asked for a story she would shake her head.

"No, I have no time for stories now. Mam lets me go to school, even though she needs my help here. When I am home there's work to do. You want stories? Come to school and learn to read and you will have all the stories you want."

Grrr! That made me so angry! I did not want to go to school. It was all right for her because she was clever and learning came easy to her. This made me feel stupid. Who did she think she was, telling me to go to school? She didn't want to tell me her stories? Well, that was fine, because I didn't want to hear them any more! So I stopped passing her cottage and I looked the other way when I saw her in the village. Sometimes I'd try to annoy her by shouting after her in my Reverend voice, "Ma-a-a-ry, Ma-a-a-ry! What did you learn in school toda-a-a-y?" She started to ignore me and that made me even more angry.

News reached our village about others who were joining the Society and the things that happened to them. Men were sent home from work and told not to return next day. Stones were thrown at people in the street of the big village. Someone had all his store of winter firewood set alight and another family found that sheep had got into their vegetable garden through a big, new hole in the fence and eaten nearly everything that was growing there. Gangs of children and some of the older boys would stand outside people's cottages, shouting and jeering. They would throw stones up on to the roofs and watch them clatter back down. Mary walked alone to school and back and sometimes, even in our little village, children shouted after her. I didn't join in the name-calling. It made me feel uncomfortable, though I was still angry with Mary.

One day I had to pass her cottage and I saw her, standing in the garden, beside the beehives. I know that they were able to earn money from selling the beeswax and the honey. Here in the village we use rush lights because they are cheap to make but rich people like beeswax candles and will pay a good price. As soon as Mary was old enough she had started to look after the bees, as well as all her other jobs. She was bending over the hives, singing softly, and I shuddered as I saw that her arms were speckled with bees. I was stung by a bee once and I can still remember the pain! How could Mary bear to have them crawling all over her?

She looked up, saw me and then looked away again. I had been thinking for many days and I knew that I needed to speak to Mary. I stopped and waited by her gate, looking over my shoulder to see if anyone was watching me.

"I have a question for you, Mary Jones," I called. She didn't look at me but I went on. "What is the difference between you and Mad Bethan? You go out walking in the dark, you talk to yourself and you do very strange things." I was looking at the bees on her arms as I said this. "How do I know you're not a witch, just like her?

How do I know you aren't as dangerous as everyone thinks you are?"

Mary gently brushed the bees from her arms and whispered something to them. Then she came over to the gate.

"First of all," said she, "You have asked me three questions." She looked at me sternly. "And, before I answer any of them I have a question for you, Bryn Parry. Why do you want to know if I am different from Bethan? I have no time for foolish questions but I'll answer if you are serious."

"I am serious. I want to understand why you and your kind do what you do. I want to decide if you are dangerous or just mad."

I could hear the "click-thunk, clack-thunk" of the loom from inside the cottage and I knew Mary was always busy, but I waited hopefully. She stopped and seemed to be thinking and then she nodded.

"All right but I shall have to be quick. Question one: there is no difference between Bethan and me, except that she is old and I am young. We are just the same. We are both people that God has made... just like you."

"Hah! But I don't go around in the dark, making magic and putting spells on people! "

"Bethan's no witch, Bryn Parry! She's just a poor, lonely old woman who brews herbs into medicine for her toothache. If you took the trouble to find the truth under the heap of lies that people talk, you'd know that!" My, she was angry but that didn't stop me.

"Huh, pretty high and mighty, aren't you? You are not my schoolmaster; talking like you know everything, 'Mary-with-your-nose-in-the-air!'"

"Anyone who walked round here with their nose in the air would soon fall into something unpleasant! I'm only telling you what is plain to see if you would only look and think! Bethan is not a witch and neither am I. You know where Mam and I go in the evenings; I told you! We meet with the Society to hear wise men read from the Bible and teach us. We go at night because we are all busy in the daytime. Your questions are just foolishness!"

I had never seen Mary like this before but I went on.

"But you talk to yourself," I said. "I've seen you. And just now you were singing to the bees! Only mad people and witches would do that."

Suddenly Mary laughed. "Oh, now I understand! It's not spells I'm muttering as I walk along or tend the bees. Sometimes I'm memorising the verses that Mr Ellis gives us and other times I'm trying to remember what I read from Mrs Pendry's Bible." She looked across at the beehives. "And there is nothing strange or witch-like in caring for bees. They will only sting you if they are afraid. If you are gentle and tell them what you are doing they will not harm you."

"But I still need to decide if you are dangerous, as people are saying."

Mary sighed and looked sad. "Is it dangerous to want to learn about God? Is it dangerous to want to read his Word? The Bible is like a light to guide us on a dark path. The more we read it and learn, the clearer we see. What harm are we doing to anyone?"

I looked away and shuffled my feet. I remembered the very first verse that Mr Ellis taught us: "Your Word is a lamp to my feet and a light to my path". I was almost satisfied with her answers, though they made me feel uncomfortable when I saw how unthinking I had been about Mad Bethan. But still I wasn't sure. If they were doing no harm to others why was our village full of worry and whispers?

Mary turned towards the hives and then looked back at me.

"You will have to decide for yourself, Bryn Parry. Use your brain and think! God gave you that brain and he will help you find the truth."

Chapter Six

I kept my eyes and ears open to what was happening around me and I heard the talk in the village. More people had joined the Society. Eli Owen and Morgan Preece from the big village had been the first but there were other names being whispered now. Other people from the villages along the valleys. Mam and the women sighed and wondered what these men were thinking of, risking their jobs for the sake of this new teaching. What were their wives supposed to feed their families on if their men had no work?

The men were more outspoken and some began to say that something must be done to stop people turning from the safe old ways.

"They need to be stopped, for their own good," said one.

"Mr Rhys reckons these fools need teaching a lesson," another said.

I thought about this and decided that they were right. Life had been quiet and happy before the new teaching started. Church was boring and meaningless but at least it kept the Reverend and Mr Rhys happy. Now we were unsettled and fearful. These people were upsetting the peaceful life of our valley by being different.

Things began to happen.

I was down in the river helping Ceris cut the rushes, ready for dipping, to make our winter's store of rush lights. We had cut a good pile and I was starting to peel them with Mam's sharp knife. When we had done this we'd carry them home and help Mam to dip them in melted mutton fat. She's been collecting the fat for months to make candles. It's a smelly job but we're all glad of a bit of light when the days grow shorter.

The children were coming home from school and I could see our Luc, wandering along, listening to Mary. Suddenly an older girl called out.

"Luc Parry! You better get away from her; she's trouble! We seen you, Mary Jones; creep-creeping about in the dark. You and your kind are not welcome here!"

Luc looked puzzled and kept walking with Mary but she whispered something to him and gently pushed him away.

"Come here, Luc!" I shouted, and I grabbed him and held him as she walked past. She was all alone and the other children were whispering and pointing, as if she was an outlandish stranger. She passed close beside me but I don't think she saw me. I saw her face and the sadness made my stomach knot but I thought maybe this was the only way to make her change her ways. Also, I was scared what the other children might do if they saw me speak to her.

* * *

*T*hings became worse after the storm. All day the clouds had gathered and built into huge, grey piles, above the mountains. The air was hot and sticky. Babies yowled and wouldn't settle. Dogs lay panting in shadows and everyone was tired and grumbling. I finished my jobs quickly and took myself off to the river, to try and keep cool. There were others there and we were pretending to be the famous Red Brigands. They used to roam the mountains here, robbing rich travellers on the lonely paths or as they forded the rivers. Despite the cool water we were soon fighting and shouting at each other over some nonsense. Then someone suddenly shouted, "Look!"

We all stopped and stared at the Mountain. Above it the sky was almost black and cloud was pouring over the summit, like porridge boiling over the edge of a pot that has been forgotten on the fire. The sun was covered and a sudden breeze made us shiver. The animals and birds fell silent and there was no sound but the chatter of the water over the river bed. We stared up at the Mountain and waited. Suddenly lightning blazed across the sky and there was a crash of thunder, like a great roar of anger.

"Run!"

We ran for home, but long before we reached our cottages we were soaked. We stayed indoors for many hours with the windows blocked and the door shut. Luc and Gwenna cried every time there was a thunder crash. Ceris tried to keep the fire burning whilst Mam walked up and down with the baby and fretted about Tada and Huw. No one dared go outside or even open the door. I sat in a corner, with my hands over my ears, and shivered. What was happening? Why had the Mountain looked so strange? What was that roaring, howling noise that sounded so like a pack of great, hungry hunting dogs?

When the storm finally passed we crept outside. The plants in our garden were flattened, thatch had been torn from the roof and some of our chickens had vanished. The pig stood in the ruins of his sty, chewing on some washing that Mam had spread to dry on a bush that morning. Huge puddles were steaming in the evening sun and the Mountain stood green and brown against blue sky. Other families had suffered the same kinds of damage as us. Everyone was talking about the storm and saying how glad they were that nothing really bad had happened. Then Tada and the men started to return with other stories.

They had taken shelter in the shepherd's huts or behind stone walls. They were all safe, but many sheep had been lost. The thunder had frightened them and they had run over a cliff or fallen in mountain streams and drowned. This was sad news, but there was worse to come. Over beyond our village, one shepherd and his family lived in a lonely cottage, on the side of the valley. When the storm started he had run home and found that part of the roof had been torn off by the wind. He had climbed up to try and stop more damage, and had fallen and broken his leg badly.

"There hasn't been a storm like this since I was a lad," one old man said. Others joined in.

"What has caused such freakish weather?"

"What have we done to deserve such ill luck?"

"Who is to blame?"

It wasn't long before the mutterings grew to an angry growl.

"Who has left the old ways? Who has turned from the ways that have always suited us? Who is following the teachings of Outsiders?"

We all knew the answer!

"Those who have meddled with the old ways have brought disaster on us! They have unleashed the Powers!" Many people looked up at the Mountain or made the sign against evil. I shivered as I remembered the cloud pouring down from the Mountain and that terrible howling sound.

As it grew dark, a crowd of the men and older boys gathered by the church. I slipped out of our cottage and followed them as they marched towards the big village. I kept back because I knew Tada would send me home if he saw me. As we walked men talked of asking the trouble-makers to change their ways and, if they refused, to leave the village and take the ill luck with them.

When they reached the big village the men joined a bigger crowd and set off along the track through the village. It was dark by now and the crowd was made of shadows, with a few lanterns to light the way. I crept closer. Soon we reached a cottage on the edge of the village. Light glowed around the shutter at the window and there was the sound of singing from inside.

The crowd stopped and shuffled about, waiting. Then a figure stepped forward and hammered on the door, shouting. Others joined in and soon the noise was deafening. I saw the door open and the shape of two men, standing with a light behind them. One man looked quite old and his hair was white. I knew the other man was Eli Owen, one of Mr Rhys' farm workers. I saw them step outside and carefully pull the door almost closed behind them. The old man stood and listened to what the leader said. Men nearby waved their arms and shook their fists and he spread his hands as if to show he had nothing to hide. Who knows what was said? The noise was so terrible that only those nearby would have heard. The shouting went on and the old man shrugged and shook his head. Then he turned back towards the door.

Suddenly someone jumped at him out of the crowd. Eli pushed the old man behind him and a fist hit him instead. The man who hit Eli was pulled back by the crowd but he struggled with them. Eli staggered but turned to face the crowd, shielding the old man behind him. He kept his hands down and I knew he wouldn't fight back. He seemed to be trying to explain but the crowd was too noisy. The man who was being held back broke free and hit him again and, this time, Eli fell. The crowd went quiet and the man who had done the hitting was pulled back again, roughly. I crept even closer, knowing that everyone was looking at the doorway and not at me. Suddenly the door opened again and some other men rushed out and pushed into the crowd. They pulled the old man back into the cottage and picked Eli up. As they carried him inside I could see blood on his clothes and running from his head. He was unconscious but still alive.

Behind the men I saw that the room was full of people, all staring out at us. An old woman was clinging to another woman. A man was comforting a woman who was crying. And there, just before the door was slammed shut, was Mary. She was crouching against the wall with her hands over her mouth. Her face was white and she looked terrified. I tried to push myself back into the crowd but I swear that, before the door was slammed shut, she saw me. The look on her face made me feel sick.

Chapter Seven

When the door slammed shut the crowd growled but then gradually went quiet. The men stood looking at the cottage, as if they didn't know what to do next. Then the leader spoke loudly.

"We have done enough for tonight, lads. Evan Harris, there was no cause for such violence!" He glared at the man who had been so quick to use his fists. "We were meant to give a clear message with no bloodshed. As it is, I think little real harm has been done. We shall leave them to think and hope that they see sense."

Heads nodded in agreement and slowly the crowd broke up. I slid back into the shadows and ran ahead so that I was safely home and in bed by the time Tada and Huw got back. Later I could hear Mam and Tada talking quietly by the fire.

"A bad business... the crowd... oh, no!... in an ugly mood... fool used his fists... could have been killed... learn their lesson ... "

I curled in a ball next to Luc and tried to sleep but I couldn't. In my mind I could see the shadowy crowd and feel the anger in it. I saw the two men come out of the cottage and stand alone, facing the crowd. I saw Eli staggering from the blow that hit him, but standing firm, not fighting back. I squeezed my eyes shut, trying to block out the sight of him falling and all those frightened people, huddled in the cottage. Most of all, Mary was there, even if I pressed my fingertips into my eyes till they ached. I kept seeing her white face and her eyes, staring and staring at me.

Next morning I crawled from bed, feeling I had ridden the Night Mare for many nights; not just the one.

"Are you sick, son?" asked Mam, looking at me closely.

"My head aches," I said, and that was true. She put a hand to my brow.

"There's no fever but your face is pale. Rest quietly for a while and we will see how you are."

I was glad to be free of questions and be excused from my jobs. I lay down again and, when everyone was busy or gone out to the fields, I slipped out of the cottage and down to a quiet stretch of the river. I needed time alone to think.

The sound of the water over the stones and the sparkle of the sunlight on the ripples soothed me. I sat watching two wagtails flicking their way from rock to rock and I thought about all that I had seen and heard.

"Use your brain and think!" Mary had said. I sat on the riverbank until the sun was high overhead and my belly told me it needed food. When I started for home I had made up my mind.

The people of the Society were not mad or evil; they were harmless. They followed new paths but these were not wicked. All the wickedness I had seen last night and in the days before had been from others, not from them. They didn't call bad names after people in the street. They didn't set fire to people's woodpiles or spoil their gardens. They didn't scare old ladies or strike out at unarmed men. Mary sometimes had a sharp tongue and I had seen her angry, but she was kind and fair. She was gentle with little children and the creatures she cared for. If she had learned these ways from the Society then they must be good people. What harm had they ever done any of us?

We feared them because they were different, but that was not a good reason for driving them away. I felt ashamed. Mary and her people were brave. They followed what they believed in, even if it meant hardship and danger. I was a lazy coward! I didn't want to be different. I believed what others said because I was too lazy to think for myself. I had joined with bullies and watched while good people were treated unfairly. But I wanted to change. From now on I would try and avoid those who made trouble. Mary was my friend and even though I didn't understand what she believed, I could watch and listen and maybe help her and her mam. If she could face an angry crowd, I wondered could I stand with her and be her friend.

$\mathscr{I}$ went to her cottage as soon as I got a chance. As you know, it stands on the track, just beyond the packhorse bridge over the river. It can be seen clearly by anyone on that part of the track or in the fields either side of the river. As I walked towards it I felt as if hundreds of eyes were watching me. Though they mostly belonged to sheep there were also some men, working in a field on the opposite hillside. Could they see me? I walked on and reached the bridge. The river was still quite high after the storm and had overflowed its banks a little. Stepping on to the bridge I could hear the sounds of voices and splashing. Looking over, I saw that part of the riverbank behind Mary's cottage had crumbled and their cow was standing in the water. Mary and her mam were trying to persuade her to climb out. The bank was churned-up mud and stones, though not too steep for old Alis to climb, but she's a stubborn creature. Mary held the halter and was pulling Alis's head while her mam had hitched up her skirts and was standing in the water, pushing from behind. It was clear to me that they needed a man's help and I was about to run over when I saw Ieuan Morris, Trefor's tada, riding towards me in his cart. I knew he had been at the trouble and that his family all spoke ill of the Society.

"Good day to you, Bryn Parry," he said as I stepped aside to let him cross the bridge. "What are you doing in these parts?"

I ducked my head and didn't look him in the eye. "Just on my way home," I mumbled.

"Hop up; I'll give you a ride," he offered. I looked across to where Mary and her mam were struggling with the cow. Ieuan looked too and a cruel smile crossed his face. "That'll keep them too busy to make more mischief," he grunted. "Well, what's keeping you, boy?"

I climbed into the back of the cart and rode home, my face burning with shame. "Coward, coward, coward!" I muttered to myself. I had only just decided to try and stand with Mary and her people and I had failed already. I was frightened of what Ieuan would think or, worse still, say about me to other people. This could not go on; I must do better. Next time I would speak openly to them and not worry who might see.

It was some time before I saw Mary again because Tada kept me busy, repairing the stone walls of sheepfold. I stuck to my decision and never joined the gossip or rude jokes about the Society members. That was easy, though. It would be harder to be seen in their company. At last I had a chance to make a visit.

When I reached the cottage Alis was tethered and grazing happily. A neighbour was driving some bullocks along the track towards me and a group of my friends were having a water fight in the river nearby but I held up my head and called out to Mary. She was sitting in the shade of the cottage wall, preparing wool for spinning; straightening the strands with quick flicks of the sharp-toothed carders. The basket at her feet was full of little soft, grey clouds of wool.

She nodded at me but her eyes were wary. It was the first time I had spoken to her since the trouble and the memories came flooding back. I hung my head and scuffed my feet in the grass but she didn't speak. Perhaps she wouldn't forgive me for being with the troublemakers? I would understand if she never wanted to speak to me again. At last I found the courage I needed.

"I have come to see how you are," I said. "After the trouble."

Mary laid down her carders and looked at her hands.

"Yes, there was trouble but all is well, thank God."

"But Eli... the man who was hurt? I thought, at first, they had killed him!"

"His head is mending; no great damage was done. Thankfully, William Huw was not harmed either."

I supposed that this was the name of the old man that Eli was protecting.

She shook her head sadly. "It seems wrong to shout in that way at such a good old man. He has done no harm and preaches only the truth."

She spoke calmly but I could not.

"It wasn't safe! What were you doing, walking to the big village in the dark and after that terrible storm, too?"

"We wanted to join with the others," she replied. "William Huw said we should meet to thank God for his protection. I know there was damage but it could have been so much worse. We were praying for those who had suffered and asking God to show us how we might help them."

"The crowd was so angry! They thought the storm came because of you. They thought it was your fault that Waldo Proctor broke his leg!"

"How is all this our fault?" she asked. I realised that there was no clear answer.

"Some people think you can make bad magic and ill-wish people," I said. "Others think that you have upset Them, up there on the mountain, by leaving the old ways."

Mary nodded and smiled. "Yes, it seems we have great power. We can make thunderstorms and cause men to fall from their roofs. Are you not fearful that maybe I will turn you into a frog or make your nose turn blue and burst?"

I laughed at this but I was amazed that she could be so calm.

"Are you not fearful of what people or... Them, up there, might do?" I asked her.

"Yes, sometimes I am afraid of what people may do," she nodded. "It is as though they are blind and cannot see what the Bible is teaching. Because they cannot see they don't understand. But you know I have no fear of those others; they belong in stories." She looked at me seriously. "We trust that God will take care of us. He knows even if a little sparrow falls to the ground and he says we are worth more than many sparrows!"

"Will you still go to your meetings, even after all that happened?"

"Of course! We have so much more to learn, and" she smiled at me. "There are so many more stories to hear!"

Mary picked up her carders and began to brush the wool again. It was time I went. I had been sent to gather firewood and so far I hadn't picked up a single twig!

"Stories?" I said, hopefully. Mary nodded.

"Many stories!" She stopped then and looked me in the eye. "Oh, but you do not go to school now, do you?"

I stared back at her but, in the end, it was I who blinked first!

I sighed. "I will come back to the school, if I must, but you will have to speak to Mr Ellis for me."

* * *

I have said that Mr Ellis was a patient man but he was also a forgiving man. I don't know what Mary said to him but when I arrived at the schoolroom, with the cleanest feet I could manage, he greeted me with a smile.

"Welcome back, Master Parry!" he said. "You are just in time. Very soon I will have to move on to another village and it may be some time before I can return. Let's see how that quick brain of yours will help you learn all I can teach you before I leave."

And so I began to learn again. This time, though, I tried harder and soon I made progress. Learning to read wasn't easy but it wasn't as hard as I had thought it would be. I was given a slate and I began to write the letters and words that I learned and Mr Ellis was pleased with me. Better than that, Mary was pleased and now she was willing to tell me all the stories that she knew. I would sit with the others in the corner of the yard as she told us about Moses the prince of a country called Egypt. How he led a huge crowd of people across a desert for forty years to a wonderful place called the Promised Land. Then there were more stories about the David who killed giant Goliath and Daniel who spent the night in a lion's den and was still alive in the morning – such exciting stories!

I liked it best when we were walking to and from school because I usually had Mary to myself. Many of the other village children still weren't allowed to walk with her, though it didn't stop them joining the group for stories once they were in the school yard! So, often it was only me, with Luc tagging along, though he didn't really count. The journeys to and from school were times when she wasn't busy working at one of her many jobs. We had the whole journey for stories and I could ask many questions, without other children interrupting.

Tada was not pleased that I was back at the school.

"'Tis a waste of time!" he grumbled. "The boy will get big ideas and think he's too good to work with the sheep and then where will he be? Reading books won't put food on the table!"

"Hush now," said Mam. "You know how much he wants to work with you and Huw at the sheep! He will join you soon, but to have someone in the family to read and write will help us all. He will understand the notices at the market and make sure we are not cheated. He will sign our name like a gentleman and you will have greater respect from those you work for and trade with."

Mam was very pleased that I was at the school again and she made sure that Tada agreed with her in the end. He had one last try, though.

"I'll not have you mixing with that little trouble-maker, Jones the weaver's daughter!" he growled at me.

"She's only a child, Madoc," Mam argued for me. "Her people may have changed their ways but they're peaceable, which is more than I can say for that fool Evan Harris and the rest of you! All that talk of bad magic is nonsense, when you see how well they have

67

behaved, even when they were threatened. They have been kind and helpful to those who suffered in the storm. What has fine Mr Rhys done to help?"

Tada looked worried and tried to hush Mam. "Hold your tongue, woman! You don't know who may be listening."

But she wouldn't be hushed. "'Tis true, I don't hold with all that they do but I think some of them have done more good for the village than that Mr Rhys has ever done! I think it may do our boy good to go to school with Mary Jones. It's well known that she is hard-working and a clever girl. They say Mr Ellis is amazed at her skill and he's a gentleman!"

After that Tada gave up for a while but I could see he was still fearful of what Mr Rhys might do if he knew that the son of one of his shepherds was spending time with a person he disapproved of. I was amazed at the change in Mam, though, and I knew things would go easier with her on my side.

Chapter Eight

For a few more weeks we went to the school and soon I was reading simple words and writing short sentences on my slate. My writing never seemed to have the neat loops and curls that others made in theirs but I was content that I could write a little. I tried to learn the verses that Mr Ellis gave us each day but only the shorter ones stayed in my memory. There was one I liked and remembered easily. It was about a shepherd. "The Lord is my shepherd, I shall lack nothing." Mr Ellis said that the "Lord" was God and that this verse meant that, like a good shepherd, God would look after us and make sure we had all we needed. I could understand about a shepherd taking good care of his sheep. Healthy sheep give good lambs and fine wool and that makes Mr Rhys happy. I wasn't sure that I liked the idea of God thinking I was a sheep. I am far cleverer than a silly sheep!

Mary was ahead of most of us. She could read nearly everything that Mr Ellis wrote on his board. She read swiftly, without stumbling or sounding out the letters like I have to do. She could repeat long passages from the Bible from memory; passages we never heard at school. I knew why she could do this. She was still visiting Mrs Pendry at the farm to read her Bible every week. All day long, whatever she was doing, she repeated and repeated what she read so that it stuck fast.

Mr Ellis was very proud of her and he would ask her to recite to us all. Mary would stand up and speak and you could see that she was very happy to do this. If someone like Trefor Morris did this he would look smug and proud because he felt he was much better than the rest of us. Some of us boys always made sure he was sorry by the time he reached home in the evening, though! But Mary; she wasn't being high and mighty. She was so enjoying the words and what they said. It was clear she wanted us to enjoy them, too.

* * *

The day came when Mr Ellis told us that he was moving on to another village to start another school.

"There are so many others who want to learn, as you have done," he said. "I shall never forget this school and the children here and I shall use your example to encourage my new pupils. Everyone can learn something, eh, Master Parry?"

Some children were very sad to hear that school would be ending. Mr Ellis promised that he would try and come back one day or send another master to teach us. I was glad to be free of the schoolroom again, though I was sorry I hadn't worked harder from the start.

As we walked home on the last day, Mary told me that she had some plans.

"While the school is closed I will help anyone who wants to learn to read," she said. "I have watched Mr Ellis closely for some time and I know his methods. I think I know enough now to teach others."

That seemed a good idea. There were more children, and even some older people, who had seen us learning and decided it was something they should do, too.

"I also have another plan," Mary added. "I've decided that I will buy a Bible."

"A Bible?" I was very surprised. "Books are not for people like us!"

Mary frowned as she trudged along the track. "I don't see why I can't have a Bible. William Huw has one that he teaches us from. Mrs Pendry has one that she and her husband read. None of them are very grand people and we are taught that God's word is for everyone!"

I thought her plan was mad. "Whatever makes you think that you could buy a Bible?" I laughed. "Books cost money; lots of money, and you don't have any!"

Mary glared at me. "Stop your laughing, Bryn Parry, or there will be no more stories!" She walked on in silence and I could see she was thinking hard. Finally she spoke again.

"If I had a Bible I could read it whenever I wanted to. All those wonderful stories! All those things that God wants to teach me! I would not have to wait till the Society meetings or when I visit Mrs Pendry at the farm," her eyes were excited. "But I don't just want it for me, though. That would be greedy. I could read it to Mam and me every day and I could read it to other people, too. I could also use it to teach people to read! Oh, it would be so good!" I had never seen Mary so excited and I felt bad that I would have to bring her feet down to the ground again.

"But where will you find this Bible you are going to buy?" I asked.

"William Huw says that sometimes they are to be bought in the town of Bala," she replied. "I shall ask him to help me find one; he is a very wise man."

"But the money," I reminded her. "How will you find the money?"

"I will find a way," she said; looking me in the eye in that way she has. "It is not impossible so I will try and I don't care what you think!"

Well, I didn't think Mary could work any harder but she did! Maybe it was just as well that school had finished because now she had more time to work. I was busy too, doing jobs for Mam. The men had taken the sheep up to the high summer pasture but Mam said I was too young to live up in the mountains with them.

"Maybe next year," she said. "But I need a man to help me here at home and Luc is still too young."

I was glad that she thought me able to do man's work and that made me feel better about being left behind.

Next year I would climb the mountain track and live in the hafod and work with Tada and Huw. I saw it whenever we walked over the hills to the market in the big town by the river. It's just an ordinary stone building but, up there, it's a lonely, special place. You are surrounded by steep grassy slopes and rocky crags. Up there the kites and buzzards live and you are so much nearer the Mountain. I wondered how it felt to live so high and if I would be fearful when the clouds came down and covered everything.

One day I got a chance to visit the hafod. Mam asked me to take some fresh bread and Tada's cloak that she had mended. It was an easy walk and the sun was shining. The Mountain looked safe today; a big green hump, covered in brown patches, like my winter blanket. This would be a good day to try and climb it, I thought but I knew I wouldn't. I had no time and, anyway, I didn't dare! I know how quickly the sun can disappear and the clouds come over. People have died up there. It's easy to lose your way when the mist covers the tracks. The wind can blow cold up there; not just in the winter either. Then there were other risks, too. I did not have Mary's certainty that They were only make-believe.

Tada was pleased to see me and Huw let me help him skin a rabbit with his new knife. I stayed and ate with the men at midday and listened to their talk while we rested from the heat. I heard a name I recognised and listened more closely.

"Yes, 'tis true. Morgan Preece went up there, after the storm, and put their roof to rights. Waldo Proctor's leg is still mending and he cannot do it. His wife told me herself."

There were murmurs of surprise.

"He went up to their cottage?"

"Mended the roof?"

I knew that Morgan was one of the men who had lost his job, along with Eli Owen. He was in the cottage when the crowd came and Eli was hurt by Evan Harris.

"Yet he's one of those trouble-makers..." someone said.

"So-called trouble-makers!" Someone interrupted him. "The very next morning, after the storm and after the, er... argument over in the big village, Morgan arrives at Waldo's door with hammer and nails and a basket of food for his family."

Men shook their heads as if this was too hard to believe. I knew it would be true, though. I had seen the kind and gentle way that Mary and her mother treated people and I was sure that the other Society members would be the same.

"Maybe we have been too quick to find fault with these people," one older man said quietly. "Such goodness could only come from a kind and forgiving heart."

* * *

*I*t was some time before I saw Mary again. One day, when I had finished all my jobs and was in no hurry to go home for more, I met her walking out of the village. She was carrying a basket on her back and it looked heavy.

"Good day to you, Mary Jones!" I said as I popped out of the bushes beside her. She stopped, with her hand over her heart.

"Bryn Parry, do you want me to die of fright?"

I tried to look sorry but it was fun to try and make people jump out of their skins!

"Where are you going with that basket?" I asked.

"To Mrs Pendry at the farm," she replied. "I am returning a great pile of mending I've done and taking her some eggs. Her hens are not laying just now. I am taking them to her because today is the day I go to read her Bible."

"I'll come with you," I said. "You can tell me a story as we walk."

"Oh, can I?" said she, as she hitched the basket higher on her shoulders. "And what will you do for me, apart from hindering me with your chatter and trying to kill me with your jumping-out?"

"Hmm, well maybe I could carry the basket some of the way?" I offered.

Mary plodded on. "And smash all my eggs before we get there? Thank you, but no!"

I was offended at this. "I can be very careful and there will be no jumping!"

So Mary handed me the basket and I carried it all the way. For this Mary told me two good stories. One was a story that Jesus told, about two men who built houses. One was on the sand, the other on a high rock. When the rain came the house on the rock stood firmly and the house on the sand was washed away. I knew that was going to happen! The other story was also about the rain. She told me of a man named Noah who built a huge boat and filled it with animals so that they would be saved from a great flood.

I was sorry when we arrived at the farm, and I decided to wait there until Mary was ready to come home. I waited a long time but then she came bouncing out of the farmhouse, looking very pleased. She opened her handkerchief and handed me one of the Welsh cakes wrapped in it.

"Mrs Pendry was so pleased with my eggs that she baked these while I read and she gave me an extra penny because she knows I am saving up for a Bible!"

"How much money have you got?" I asked.

"I have three pennies and five half-pennies and two farthings," she said proudly. I was impressed.

"That is a good amount of money to have already. You must keep it safe."

"Oh yes, I do. I have a wooden box that Mam gave me and all my Bible money goes in there."

"Hm, but you still need a lot more. I should think that a Bible will cost many shillings."

Mary nodded. "Yes, so I must keep saving."

We ran most of the way home because the basket was empty. Mary had just started to teach me the next part of "The Lord is my shepherd" when she stopped and pointed at the ground.

"Look!"

There on the track, just in front of us, lay a money purse. I ran, picked it up and shook it. It was heavy and it jingled."

"Oh, my! Here's some more money for your Bible!" I shouted.

Mary shook her head. "It's not mine," she said. "Someone has lost it and will be worrying. We must hurry and find the owner."

I sighed. Why did she have to be so good? It seemed a shame when she needed the money. But I had to agree that the right thing would be to find the owner.

We passed no one on the track and when we got back to Mary's cottage, she went up to the cottages nearby and I ran on down the track to the church. I was nearly home when I saw a man, leading his horse, and walking slowly towards me. He was looking this way and that, all along the track.

"Sir, have you lost something?" I asked.

"Indeed I have," said he, looking most anxious. "I was returning over the hill from the town, where I had sold two fine bullocks. Now I find I've dropped my purse and all the money in it."

"Come with me!" I shouted and hurried him back up the track, calling for Mary as I went. When he saw what Mary held he smiled till I thought his face would split!

"Thank you!" he said, and then he put his hand into the purse and held up a whole sixpenny piece! "Take this with my thanks," he said as he dropped it into Mary's hand. We stood and stared at it as he rode away. Neither of us had ever been so close to so much money before. Mary handed it to me.

"We should share it," she said.

"But you found the purse," I replied.

"You found its owner, though."

I thought about this and all the things I could buy with three whole pennies. Then I handed it back to her.

"No, you should have it for the Bible." I said. "You said that you'll share it with other people so I will put my three pence to the collection as long as you read me lots of stories!"

Mary smiled. "You'll be able to read them for yourself by the time I have all the money I need."

Chapter Nine

A long time passed. Ceris wed Ieuan Griffith and that meant I was the oldest child left at home to help Mam when Tada and Huw were away. No one came to reopen the school but Mary and some of the other clever children would sometimes meet and practise their reading and writing. The rest of us just joined them for Mary's story-telling but she made us earn our stories. We had to memorise the verses that she knew or practise our letters in the dust. Parents seemed happy for their children to mix with Mary now. Even some of those who had earlier been suspicious of the Society members spoke more gently about them. Everyone had heard about how Morgan Preece had helped Waldo Proctor and his family after the storm.

Word had got around that Mary was saving for a Bible and there were some who admired her for what she was doing. They found her jobs to do and paid more generously than they needed to for the work she did. My first question whenever I met her was, "How much money have you, now"? Slowly, very slowly, her box was filling with money, but she still didn't have enough.

One day, Owen the Pack came through the village. As soon as we heard, we children all hurried down to meet him. Mam and the women came more slowly, for the news he'd tell and to see what he was carrying.

Glynis and Trefor Morris always had money to spend and we watched as they chose what to buy this time. Glynis bought a painted wooden doll and I could see our Gwenna's eyes look lovingly at it. Trefor bought a whistle and a twist of toffees. He popped one in his mouth at once and looked round at the rest of us with a nasty smile. I thought he would need to get home quickly before one of us knocked that smile off his face and helped him eat his toffees!

Mam traded some eggs for currants so I knew that she would be baking us something sweet to eat. There was no money for us to buy treats, though. I thought of Mary and her money box and wondered what I would do if I had some money saved.

She stayed away when Owen the Pack called and I thought that I would have to do the same. I was certain that I wouldn't be able to resist some of the lovely things he had in his pack. If I had a money box it would be empty most of the time!

I was sad for Mary. Even before she started to save for her Bible she and her mam never had any money for treats. Now she had some money but she still had no treats. Having a Bible must be very important to her. Why else would she go without things when she had the money to buy them?

"Trefor Morris has toffees," I told her later that day. "Though he's such a greedy pig he may have eaten them all by now."

"Mam says that toffees stick to your teeth and sometimes pull them out," she said as she scattered grain for her hens. I laughed at the thought of Trefor the Pig with no teeth.

"Serve him right!"

Then I remembered some news I had heard.

"Owen the Pack says that there's much talk about a preacher who lives in Bala and is turning the town upside down."

Mary stopped and looked at me.

"I think he's talking of the Reverend Thomas Charles," she said, looking excited. "William Huw has been to Bala and heard him preach. He is a great man of God!"

I shrugged. If he was anything like our Reverend I didn't think he would be anything to get excited about. Also, Bala is a town that is so far away that it might as well be on the moon!

"Why should we be interested in this Reverend? What has he got to do with us?" I asked.

"It was the Reverend Charles who sent Mr Ellis to be our schoolmaster," said Mary. "I heard that at our meeting one time."

This was interesting. "But why did he want to start a school here, in the middle of the mountains; we aren't a grand town like Bala?"

"William Huw said that he was sad that so many people here can't read. He wants every one to learn so that each life will be better. But, most of all, he wants people to learn about God by reading the Bible. He has started schools in many places."

"Huh! You knew all about this and you didn't tell me?" I said.

"I didn't think it would interest you," she replied.

I was disappointed because I thought I was bringing her news she didn't know. Then I remembered something else.

"Ah, but did you know that this famous Reverend has been seen, travelling the hills and valleys around these parts... on a white horse?"

That made her eyes pop!

"The Reverend Charles is coming here!" Her face was pink with excitement.

"I didn't say that! I said he'd been seen around these parts."

Mary took no notice. "Weeks ago, William Huw said at the meeting that the Reverend Charles was planning to visit the Societies, here in the valleys. If Owen the Pack has heard this it must mean he is getting nearer. I must tell Mam."

She hurried back to her cottage and I was left, still wondering what was so exciting about a Reverend who rode a white horse.

* * *

Not long after that something happened that put thoughts of Reverends and white horses out of my head.

Sunday morning we were all squashed into our pew in the church, as usual. I was wearing a new shirt that Mam had made. It was a very fine shirt, just like Tada wears, but the cloth was still stiff and it rubbed my neck and wrists. It was hard not to fidget and Mam had already pinched me twice to make me sit still. I was twisting and turning my head to ease my sore neck when I saw something out of the corner of my eye.

In the wall beside our pew is the old leper's window. It was set crooked into the wall, long ago, so that the poor outcasts could watch the pulpit and hear the service without coming near the healthy people. There are no lepers now but I was sure I saw a strange, pale face looking in through the window. Mam's elbow nudged me in the ribs and I turned back to look at the Reverend, who was baa-baa-ing at the front. I tried to turn my eyes back to the window, without moving my head too much, and then I jumped!

There was the face, peering through the window. It was old and ugly. I was surprised but not frightened because the face looked ill and so sad. When I jumped the Reverend looked over at our pew and Mam pinched me again, hard! Luc and Gwenna started to fidget then and people turned around. Tada's face grew very red and I knew there would be trouble later. What was the Reverend doing? I watched as he frowned at the window and flicked his hand, as if he was shooing something away. At the end of the service I turned and looked and the face at the window had gone.

After we had eaten our dinner I went along the river. It was a cold day but I wanted to be out of the cottage and away from my family. My backside hurt from the beating Tada had given me, even though I tried to explain about the face at the window. Coming towards me along the track were Mary and her mam. I knew they would not have been working on their vegetable patch because the Society members are just as strict as we are about not working on the Sabbath.

"Good day to you Bryn Parry," said Mary's mam.

"You'll likely be needing a cushion to sit on this afternoon?" said Mary with a little smile. I don't understand how news gets around this village so fast. Good or bad, everyone knows your business in no time.

"Hush, Mary!" said her mother, though she was smiling, too.

I put my hands in my pockets and pretended I didn't know what they were talking about. Mary's mam hurried on and Mary walked with me.

"You saw her, didn't you?" she said.

I shrugged but didn't answer.

"It was poor Bethan," Mary went on. "She's sick and needed comfort so she went to the church."

"Why didn't she come inside like everyone else?"

"Because she doesn't feel welcome."

I remembered the Reverend's angry flick of the hand and I understood.

"We have been to her cottage with food and Mam is going home to fetch a blanket. She will go back later and sit up with her tonight. I am going to fetch firewood; the poor soul has none and her cottage is so cold."

I went with her and together we collected a big pile of firewood. We took it to Mad Bethan's cottage and I lit the fire while Mary put a pot of water on to boil. Soon her mam returned with food and blankets and made the old woman comfortable. She spoke gently as Mam does to the baby when it cries.

"Go home, now," she said to Mary. "There's work to do at home. The animals will need tending before dark. God go with you and keep you safe."

We hurried back together and I fed the pig and collected in the hens for the night while Mary milked the cow. It was almost dark when I got home and I pictured

Mary, all alone in her cottage with only a cat for company. I thought about her mam's kindness to poor old Mad Bethan. I was glad that I had been able to help, too, and it made me feel a bit better about my sore backside.

Chapter Ten

The next morning everyone knew that it was Mad Bethan's face at the leper's window that had disturbed the church service. They knew, too, that she was sick. Everyone had an opinion about what had caused her sickness.

"She's old. The old get sick and die; 'tis the way of things."

"She strayed too far, the old fool! I saw her, up there on the Mountain, gathering things."

"T'is common knowledge that They punish those who climb too high and take what isn't theirs."

"I heard the Hounds baying last night. Someone will die soon, be sure of it!"

It was strange that everyone was so interested in Mad Bethan's health when usually no one noticed her much at all. I thought it was sad, though, that the only people to help her were Mary and her mam.

Mary's mam spent all her time with Mad Bethan and Mary ran between the two cottages, taking food and other things that were needed. When I had time, I helped to gather more firewood and feed Mary's hens.

"Why do you spend so much time with those people?" Mam asked.

"They have too much work to do, now that they are caring for Mad Bethan," I said. I was afraid she would stop me by giving me more work to do.

"I only go when I have finished my work here," I said quickly.

Mam smiled. "Go, I'll not stop you. They are good people, I see that, but don't let your Tada find out!"

I was glad that Mam's heart was softening and I made sure that I did her jobs without complaining.

As I said, though, there were others whose hearts had not changed. Many were still sure that she was sick because she had done something wrong.

"Mam says Mad Bethan is sick because she made Them angry," said Trefor Morris when he saw me one day. He looked towards the Mountain and he smiled as though he was enjoying the thought. I was passing him with my arms full of firewood, otherwise I would have been very happy to knock that smile off his face!

"You know nothing, pig!" I said and I hurried on. But I looked upwards and shivered. The cloud was low on the Mountain and there was already a sprinkling of snow. What if Trefor's mam and those others were right? What if Mad Bethan was being punished by Them? I wished I could be sure that They had no power.

I took the wood to Mary's cottage and went inside to put it by the fireplace. I was surprised to see Mary and her mam were both there. They were sitting by the fire with their heads bowed as we do in church when the Reverend is praying. Mary's mam looked up at me.

"She's gone, God rest her soul," she said quietly. She looked at the wood I had brought. "Thank you, lad. You have a kind heart." Then she got up and went to the chest in the corner.

"I have a just finished a new length of cloth here that will do well to wrap her in. I shall take it now and do what's needed before William Huw and the others arrive for the burying." She tucked it inside her cloak and laid a hand on Mary's head as she left. "See to the animals, my dear, and I'll return soon."

Mary nodded and then sighed sadly, as we went outside to feed the hens.

"Why did Mad Bethan die?" I asked. Mary turned on me, her eyes flashing.

"For the last time, Bryn Parry, SHE IS NOT MAD!"

I stepped back in surprise and then watched as Mary burst into tears.

"She never did anyone any harm. She was just old and lonely. They could have made her last days happy but people chose to believe lies about her instead of being good neighbours." She rubbed her eyes with her sleeve.

"People are saying—"

"Oh, I know what people say!" she said angrily. "All that talk of Them on the Mountain; it's all rubbish! She just caught a chill in the rain and was too weak to recover. It's not a very exciting reason but it's the truth."

I really wanted to believe she was right. She looked at me and gave a little smile.

"Forgive me, Bryn Parry. I lose patience quickly and I must try harder to control it but sometimes people's foolishness makes me so angry!"

I fed the pig and Mary went to milk the cow. I wondered if there was something else I could do.

"Poor soul; she has no family to mourn her," Mary said, as she leaned against the cow's side. "The men from the Society will be the only ones to commit her to God's safe keeping."

Then I knew what I could do to show her I was different from the others.

"I will go to the burying," I said.

Her smile made her face shine. "Bryn Parry, that is a very good idea!"

* * *

A burying is men's work. I had watched others from a distance but this was the first time I had been part of the group. This time I followed as the men carried Bethan's coffin to the churchyard. I don't know who paid for her coffin, but I was glad that she was wrapped warmly in the new cloth that Mary's mam had woven. When we arrived I stood behind the circle of men around the grave but they moved aside and drew me in. I recognised Eli Owen and Morgan Preece and I realised that the old, white-haired man must be William Huw. I had last seen him in the dark at the trouble in the big village.

The Reverend did his part quickly and hurried away without speaking to any of us. I expect he wanted to get out of the cold and he had no time for Bethan even when she was alive. The rest of us stayed, and William Huw stepped to the graveside. He spoke kindly of Bethan and his prayers were full of the love that God has for his creatures. He said that Bethan was now in the care of the Good Shepherd and her suffering was over. I remembered the shepherd verses that Mary had taught me and I was glad to think that God would not shoo Bethan away as the Reverend had done.

The men sang a song I did not know so I kept my head bowed and I said sorry to Bethan for calling her mad. Then I marched back through the village with the men and I didn't care who saw me!

* * *

*A*fterwards, people talked about the death of Bethan for a while. They kept on with their talk of Them and the Mountain, too. I was afraid that the people of the Society would have more trouble because of their dealings with her. But most people were impressed that the Society members were willing to help someone that they hardly knew. I could feel that more hearts were softening. Tada got to hear of me going to the burying and I waited for the beating he would give me but none came.

"You are almost a man now, son," he said. "You must make your own choices. If Mr Rhys questions me I shall tell him that I'm no longer responsible for your actions."

I think maybe he was impressed by the Society people, too, but he wasn't ready to say so, for fear of what might happen. I worked hard when I was with him, to show how responsible I could be and I waited to see what would happen next.

* * *

One day in spring I met Mary, dashing along the track to the village. She was full of excitement. The wind was wild and whipped our clothes and hair about. It threw showers of rain at us and tried to snatch away our words. We had to shout to be heard.

"Good day to you, Mary Jones!" I shouted. She pulled her shawl tighter around her shoulders and stepped off the track and into the shelter of a big tree.

"Bryn Parry, you will never guess who I have met!" Her eyes were shining and she was smiling widely. I knew this must mean that she was talking about a good Someone and not Giant Idris or another like him. I didn't need to wait because she went on, quickly.

"Today, as usual, I walked to the farm to take Mrs Pendry's mending and read her Bible. I was nearly there when I met a rider on the track. He was a gentleman, wrapped in a big cloak, against the rain and he was riding a white horse!"

Mary stopped and waited to see if I understood.

"A white horse?" I asked. "Do you mean it was...?"

"Yes! It was the Reverend Thomas Charles himself! He was riding over to the big village and tonight he will speak at the meeting in William Huw's house."

Well, I couldn't see what there was to get so excited about. One Reverend is the same as another, surely? I realised she had more to say, so I let her tell me what had happened.

"When he saw me he stopped his horse and spoke to me. 'Where are you going girl, in this foul weather?' says he.

"'To Pendry's farm, sir, to read the Bible,' I told him.

"'Why are you going so far to do that?'

"Well, I explained to him, 'We have no Bible at home and there is none nearer. I have been saving every penny for a long time now, and I think I have enough to buy my own Bible by now, but I don't know where I can get one.'

"He smiled down from his horse and said 'Well, as it happens, I am expecting some Welsh Bibles from London before long. If you bring your money to Bala I will give you one.'"

Mary hugged her shawl tighter and her feet seemed to be trying to dance. I could see that this was very exciting news for her and I was pleased that she had finally got enough money.

"Your William Huw was right then," I said. "There are Bibles to be had in Bala.

Mary nodded. "Yes! So now I know what I shall do."

I looked at her and shook my head slowly.

"You're never thinking of going to Bala?" I asked.

"Of course I am!" she laughed.

"But it's miles and miles away! How will you know the road? What if you get lost? There may be robbers! It won't be safe!"

Mary laughed again. "What an old woman you are, Bryn Parry! Bala is not so very far away and God will go with me." She looked at my disbelieving face and stamped her foot.

"I'm going, Bryn Parry and that is that. If there are Bibles to be had then I will go... I must go!"

Chapter Eleven

"You're mad! How can you go to Bala, all alone?"

"Why shouldn't I? My feet and legs have carried me many miles already. I know I can do it."

"Yes, but you're only... a girl!"

"Ha! Say that again, Bryn Parry and I'll tell my bees to pay you a visit!"

We had many arguments like this after Mary decided she was going to Bala. Nothing I said would make her change her mind. She had an answer for every problem I thought of and I could see it was useless to try and talk her out of her idea. When I found out that her mam knew of her plan and had agreed she could go, I gave up.

"Have it your own way, Miss 'I-can-do-anything'!" I sighed. "But I still think you're mad. Walking all that way, just for a book?"

Mary laughed and went on with her work. But I knew she was making plans and I watched and listened. I needed to know what she was doing because I was making plans too.

* * *

Long ago, after the trouble in the big village, I had decided that I would help Mary and her mam whenever

I could. So now I realised that I would have to go to Bala with Mary. Someone had to make sure she got there and back again safely. I didn't really want to do it but I felt I must. I wasn't even sure how I would do it. I had no idea how to get to Bala and I feared that I wasn't as brave as Mary seemed to be. Bala might not be on the moon but it was further away than I had ever travelled, and who knew what dangers lay on the road between our little village and that town?

I wasn't foolish enough to tell Mary what I was planning to do. I knew she would never agree to me going with her. Maybe it was because she had no brothers and sisters or because she and her mam had to do everything themselves, but Mary seemed quite happy to do things alone. I knew, too, that she would worry that I might get into trouble from my family. So I said nothing but I watched and waited and hoped I would find out when she was going to make her journey.

As spring passed the days grew longer and Tada make his plans to move up to the hafod again. Mam felt Luc and Gwenna were still too young to give her the help she would need now that Ceris had her own home to keep. So I was to stay back at home for another year.

"Aw, Mam!" I moaned. "I'll be an old man before you let me go."

"Luc is still a child; he doesn't have your strength yet," said Mam and I felt proud, despite my disappointment. "You shall go up to the hafod more often this year, I promise. There are times when they will need all the hands they can find, I'm sure."

I had to be content with that promise. Then I realised that this arrangement might suit my plans. It might be very useful to have two places where I could be. Those at home would think I was at the hafod and those up at the hafod would think I was at home!

* * *

$\mathscr{A}$t last the time came when Mary told me she was leaving for Bala the next morning. The days were at their longest and the weather was good so I could see that this was the best time to go. I listened to her plans and watched as she prepared but I didn't look too interested: I didn't want her to become suspicious.

"Tomorrow I will leave at first light," she said. "Mam has made me a new bag and it will hold my food and my money. I shall take my clogs, too, for I may need them. Come and see."

I went back to their cottage and Mary showed me the new bag. I watched as her mam pushed the precious money pouch and then the bread and cheese, wrapped in a cloth, down into the front pocket of the bag. After that, she put Mary's clogs into the back pocket. When she slung it over Mary's shoulder the two halves hung down, nicely balanced. She smiled and nodded.

"That will do well, my dear," she said, looking very satisfied.

"Mam has given me her warm shawl to wear, in case the weather changes and now I am ready," Mary added. She looked so excited but also a little anxious, I thought.

"Bala is so far away," I reminded her.

"I know that, well enough!" she said sharply. Then she smiled. "I am sorry, Bryn Parry. My feelings are all mixed. I am excited and fearful and I cannot believe that I am really going to Bala at last!"

I wished her well and hurried off to make my own preparations. It would be hard for me to find food to take. In our home there are never any leftovers, except what only the pig will eat. I would be lucky if I found anything. I also needed to be very careful to get away from home next morning without too many questions.

At our evening meal I ate little and hid all my bread and cheese inside my shirt. Then, before we settled to sleep, I told Mam that I wanted to go up to the hafod to see Tada and Huw. It was a risk but I had been helpful and uncomplaining for many days, and I hoped Mam would agree.

"Yes, lad, you can go, but take some food because they may not have enough to spare for another mouth."

More food; I couldn't believe my luck!

* * *

The next morning I got up before it was light, tied the food in a bundle and crept out of the cottage. The birds were singing loudly, though the sun was still behind the mountains, and there was a light rain falling. Everything was covered in a cool, grey mist. I ran all the way to Mary's cottage and crept up to the door to listen. There were little rustling sounds and quiet voices coming from inside. Good, she was still there.

I hid in the trees nearby and waited. Soon the door opened and Mary and her mam came out. Mary was carrying her new bag and had her mam's shawl wrapped around her. Her mam kissed her and then Mary set off down the track towards the church. Her mam stood watching and waving until she was out of sight. I had to wait until she went back inside the cottage before I could follow. If she saw me word might get back to Mam that I was walking in the wrong direction for the hafod!

Again I ran, with my bundle banging against my leg. I knew the track she would take so I wasn't worried about the first part of the journey. Later I would need to keep her in sight at any meeting of tracks. At the church, Mary turned on to the narrow track that led up between two hills and over to the valley where the long lake lay. The big village was also in this valley but we didn't use this track to reach it because it was quicker to go past the ruined castle. A stream ran beside us and I hoped its chatter would cover any sound my feet made. The first part was through trees and it was easy to follow and not be seen. Now and then I saw the flick of her skirt or the sole of her foot, just ahead of me in the trees. Then the track passed through an open valley. Now I let Mary walk far ahead. I was ready to drop to the ground or hide in a bush if she turned around. The track dipped down gently and I could see that we were travelling along the side of the big valley now. I turned and saw, further back, the roofs of the big village, with smoke starting to curl up from the chimneys to join the mist. Behind us lay our homes and all the things that we knew and understood. Ahead, everything was unknown.

Mary walked fast and she didn't look back. That was good because it was sometimes still hard to find cover. Through more woods we walked, high along the side of the valley. We passed a farm where a dog ran out, barking. I had to hide behind a wall until Mary was out of sight. I could see that it wasn't going to be as easy as I'd thought to follow her all the way to Bala without being seen. But then the weather began to help me.

We had nearly reached the end of the long lake that lies in this valley. The sky was lighter, but the sun was still hidden in cloud. Then the mist rolled down from the mountains and covered everything in a wet, white blanket. This happens here sometimes, even in summer, and it is the reason our sheep always have such good green grass to eat. The rain fell harder now and I saw

Mary pull her shawl over her head. I decided it was safe to follow more closely because she would only see in front of her now. There was no danger of her catching sight of me from the corner of her eye. As we reached the end of the lake I looked up and saw, through a ragged hole in the mist, the dark shoulders of the Mountain towering above the track. I shivered at the thought of how close we were to Them. A trickle of rainwater ran down my neck like a cold finger and I almost cried out. Then the mist grew thicker, and suddenly I couldn't see Mary any more.

I crept along, following the track as well as I could. My feet slipped on wet rocks and I sank up to my ankles in boggy patches. Now and then I saw a footprint, slowly filling with water, and I knew Mary was still ahead of me somewhere. I was feeling very wet by now and hungry, too, but I didn't dare stop in case I lost Mary for good. As I stumbled along I asked myself, over and over, why someone should want to do this. What was so important about this book that you would be willing to get wet and cold and, yes, frightened too? If I had been sure of the way back I think, at that moment, I would have turned around and run home for breakfast!

Suddenly, somewhere in the mist, I heard a voice. It was Mary, I was sure, because what I could hear was the psalm about the Lord God being a shepherd. I hurried towards the sound and at last I saw her figure just ahead of me. She was sitting on a rock, tying on her clogs. One of my feet was sore from a sharp stone but I had no clogs and I am not old enough to have strong boots like Tada. I was busy thinking about how good it would be to have boots and about the rain that was running down the back of my neck and I was not walking carefully, so suddenly I slipped and fell. I picked myself up quickly and saw Mary standing, staring back at me, her eyes big and round with fear. I realised that she couldn't see me properly and would be wondering who was following her in the mist. I staggered towards her, and she sighed with relief when she saw who it was.

"Bryn Parry, you will be the death of me, I'm sure!" She looked at me sternly. "What are you doing here?"

"I've come to look after you," I said.

I was dripping and shivering and rubbing my knee. She looked at me and smiled a little.

"You seem to be having enough trouble looking after yourself!"

I was very annoyed at this. "I am cold and wet and my knee hurts. The mist is so thick I can see nothing and I have had no breakfast. This is all because I thought you needed someone to protect you!"

For a moment I thought she was going to laugh at me but she didn't.

"Thank you, Bryn Parry; you are very kind," she said. "It is a lonely road, here in the mist and it will be good to have company. We must keep moving, though. The rain may chill us and we have such a long way to go. There's a danger we will still be walking when the daylight goes and then we may lose our path."

Chapter Twelve

I was glad that we were walking together now. The path was steep and the mist still swirled around us. Through gaps in the mist I saw, high above us, black crags that were glistening with rain. I heard the sighing and moaning of the wind and shuddered. Even when I couldn't see it, I knew that up above us in the mist, the Mountain was frowning down on us. The path was clear enough most of the time, but we couldn't see far ahead and so we had to go slowly. Mary plodded on steadily and I followed close behind. I am strong and I can walk the mountains like any shepherd but fear seemed to make me weak. The rain had soaked my clothes and now many icy fingers ran down my back. Every sharp sound made me jump and look around and I was sure Mary must be able to hear the hammer of my heart.

"Ow-ooooooooo!"

The howling sounded very near and my legs felt like they were made of butter. Before I could stop myself I screamed.

"Aagh!"

Mary turned back and I grabbed her arm.

"It's the Hounds!" I shouted. "They're out hunting! We must have strayed on to the Mountain! They're coming for us! We're going to die... !"

"Bryn Parry, stop that at once!" Mary spoke sharply and shook my shoulders. "No one is coming for us, we are safe on the track and what you hear is just a dog that is shut in and wanting to be outside."

I felt ashamed but I couldn't stop shaking. The mist and the nearness of the Mountain and now the howling were all too much for me. Mary pulled me along behind her until a building loomed out of the mist. We had reached a lonely cottage.

"We'll stop here and eat," she said. She knocked at the door and when a woman answered she asked for shelter. The woman was amazed to see us dripping in her doorway and asked us in by the fire. We had our own food but she gave us some milk to drink. Sure enough, it was her dog that was howling in the outhouse. Her man was out with the older dog and this young one was pining to join them.

"You're going to Bala?" the woman asked in surprise. "My, that is a long journey. What takes you all that way on a day like this?"

Mary explained that we were going for a Bible and that we had to go, whatever the weather. "The Bibles are arriving soon and we must be in Bala when they do."

It was good to eat and be warm again and soon I felt much braver. Even so, it was hard to go out into the rain once more.

As we plodded on uphill Mary started to say the shepherd psalm again. She repeated each line so I could say it with her. Soon I knew it all through. Somehow it made me feel better as we shouted it loudly to the mist and rocks.

"Even though I walk through the valley of the shadow of Death I will fear no evil, for you are with me!"

"The Lord God is with us as we walk up this track," Mary panted, as the track grew steeper. "And you have no need to fear those things that others fear, Bryn Parry. We are safe in his hands."

Not long after this the mist began to lift and the rain stopped. When we turned around we could look back and begin to see how far we had come. Behind us the valley and its lake lay, far below us. The Mountain was behind us, too, and now our path was gentler.

"I have never been so far from the village before," I said.

"Neither have I," said Mary. "But we don't have time to stand and stare; we still have many miles to cover."

So we turned our backs on the Mountain and finished the climb out of the valley. As we forded a stream the sun came out at last. Then we reached a place where our track met another and we had to choose from two directions. Which way should we go? This way, that way? Mary stopped for a moment and looked about her, then she turned east. We walked a little way along this new track with Mary searching the woods that we passed. Then she found what she was looking for and turned off the track and on to yet another one. Now we walked across open fields.

"Are you sure this is the right track?" I was worried.

"This is the path that William Huw told me of," Mary answered. "But we will ask the next person we meet, just to be sure." Some time afterwards we reached a small village and, when we asked a man who was chopping wood, he pointed down the track we were taking.

"Now that we can see where we're going it will be easier," said Mary, and she stopped to take off her clogs. I knew she wanted to save them. Once they were worn out, how long would it be before she was able to buy another pair?

The track was grassy and soft to our feet, and the sun was hot now and high in the sky. I laughed to see the way our wet clothes were steaming.

"We look like dumplings cooked in a cloth when Mam fishes them out of the pot."

Mary laughed and unwrapped her shawl. "Oooh, don't talk about dumplings!" she said. "It makes me feel hungry and we must make sure our food lasts."

We jogged down and along the side of a wider valley; through woods and across streams. The track was now wider, too.

"This is an important track," Mary explained. "It stretches from Bala to the town by the sea, where Mr Ellis comes from. He told me about it."

This made me feel happier. We wouldn't get lost on a track like this. We began to meet more people now; coming and going along the track. When we stopped to eat, we watched as a string of packhorses plodded by. Mary kept looking at the sun, and I knew she was wondering how far we still had to go. We didn't stop often and then only for a drink at a stream. When the track went downhill we ran and when it was steep and uphill we plodded together. Mary telling me stories, if she had the breath.

All afternoon we walked and the valley grew wider and the hills lower. It felt strange, and I missed our mountains. My legs and feet were starting to feel tired but Mary said nothing, so neither did I. When the sun was starting to drop lower in the sky we walked out of a small wood and stopped to stare. There, in the distance, was a gleam of water.

A carrier's cart came towards us and the driver greeted us.

"What is that water we can see?" I asked him.

"That's Bala lake," he said. "Walk swiftly and you'll be there well before nightfall."

We were encouraged by that and set off again, thinking we were nearly there. But at that moment three horsemen burst out of the trees ahead of us. They didn't slow down and galloped at us.

"Out of the way, fools!" one of the men shouted and I pulled Mary off the track, just in time. As they passed, one of the horses brushed us aside and we tumbled into the stream that ran beside the track.

I climbed back on to the track and cursed the riders with all the worst words I could remember. Then, I looked around for Mary. She was sitting by the side of the stream, holding her hand and her face was white.

"Are you hurt?" I asked. I was angry that, yet again I had been no use to her. A fine protector I was!

"My hand twisted as I fell," she said. I jumped down beside her. I could see by her face that her hand was painful.

"Huh! They seemed to think that they owned the track," I growled.

"At least neither of us hurt a leg or a foot," she said, as she knelt to hold her wrist under the water for a while. She was putting on a brave face but I could see that she was upset.

"Yes, that would have been difficult," I agreed. "But we are going to Bala, come what may." I thought for a moment. "Hm, I wonder how long it would take us to hop there?" She laughed at that.

"I'm very glad you are here, Bryn Parry," she said.

I helped her back on to the track, and made her a clumsy sling for her arm out of the shawl. Then we went on, nearer and nearer to the lake. The sun was lower in the sky now and the shadows were growing longer. There were less people on the track too and I began to think of our cottage and the smell of cooking. I was very tired now. Never mind; we'll soon be in Bala, I thought.

Trees closed in along the track and stretched their branches overhead so that it seemed as though we walked through a tunnel. The sun's warmth could not reach us here and I shivered. I was reaching into my bundle for a bit of bread when I saw two figures slip like shadows out of the trees and on to the track ahead of us. They walked towards us, slowly. I have seen the fur on the back of a dog's neck stand up when it is threatened and I could feel the hairs on my own neck begin to prickle. These figures were different from the others we had met that day. Something told me to be wary.

"Walk behind me," I said quietly to Mary. She looked startled but, for once, she didn't argue.

I walked ahead, with my bundle over my shoulder and one hand in my pocket, whistling and trying to look as if I hadn't noticed the figures ahead of us. All the time I was searching the track for useful sticks or stones.

When they were very close the larger figure barred the way and we had to stop.

"Good day to you, travellers," he said. I looked him over and saw that he was only a little older than me and his companion was younger and smaller and had a twitch in his face. They were skinny and dirty and the older one carried a big stick. Singly I could have beaten them off but there were two of them!

"Good day to you," I replied warily.

"And where might you be going on this fine afternoon?" the older boy spoke again, showing a mouthful of crooked and broken teeth. Mary moved out from behind me, though I tried to keep in front of her.

"We go to Bala, to b—," she began.

"We go to Bala to visit our uncle," I said, and I took Mary's good arm and squeezed it hard. I hoped Mary would not correct me because I guessed that it would be dangerous to tell them about buying the Bible. If they knew we had money there would be trouble.

"All the way to Bala, eh?" said Crooked Teeth. "You look tired and you still have a long journey ahead of you. Why not stop and take a rest? We know a good place where you can sit and take your ease, don't we?" He grinned at his companion.

"Aye, that we do," the other agreed, circling us, his eyes flickering this way and that as if he didn't want to miss anything.

"Thank you but no," I replied firmly. "We need to get on."

I tried to pass Crooked Teeth but he stepped in front of me again.

"Your sister is injured and she really needs to rest!" he said, gripping my shoulder and giving me a long, hard stare.

Twitchy took hold of Mary and tried to pull her off the track, towards the trees. She gasped and looked back at me with wide eyes. Although it was cool here under the trees I could feel the sweat starting to run down my brow and inside my shirt. If it had been just me I was sure I could have dealt with them or at least outrun them, but there was Mary to consider. She was tired and injured and I must look after her. They seemed to be unarmed, apart from the stick, but I couldn't be sure. It would be dangerous to threaten them but I needed to show that I wasn't afraid. If I acted unconcerned and could convince them that we carried nothing to interest them, then we might get away unharmed. I must be very careful, though. These two were like hungry dogs that would keep sniffing around us until they got something.

"Thank you for your thoughtfulness," I said quickly, hoping my voice sounded calm and cheerful. "But we are expected in Bala today. If we delay our uncle will worry and come searching for us, in fact he may already be on his way." I stared back at him, without blinking, which is something I am good at, as you know.

Crooked Teeth thought for a moment and then dropped his hand from my shoulder and shrugged.

"Oh well, it's your loss." He seemed about to step aside and I relaxed, which was a mistake. He was waiting for this and, as I went to move around him, he stepped forward, even closer to me, crooking his arm around my neck. He smelt foul and I tried to back away from his reeking breath. He nodded to Twitchy who pushed Mary back towards us. She stumbled and caught a handful of my shirt to save herself from falling. I could feel her shaking.

"Not so fast, my friends!" continued Crooked Teeth. "First let us see what you carry in your bags." Twitchy started to pull Mary's bag from her shoulder.

"No!" She cried, gripping it hard. I had to think quickly. I knew she would never let go of that bag without a struggle. I managed to slip my bundle from my shoulder and pushed it towards Crooked Teeth, who still held me close.

"We only have some food, and little of that now," I replied instead of Mary, hoping to distract them from her bag until I could think of something.

"I have my clogs, too," said Mary in a shaking voice. My heart sank and I glared at her. Why couldn't she just keep quiet? Next she'd be offering to give them all her hard-earned money!

"Food, eh?" said Crooked Teeth and he relaxed his grip a little. I saw again how thin and hungry they both looked and an idea came to me.

"Yes," I said, trying to smile cheerfully. "Mam's home-baked bread with a crisp crust; the best bread in the village! Oh, and some very fine cheese!"

"There are two apples left as well, and a piece of bara brith, I think," said Mary quietly. I could see that she understood what I was doing and was playing along.

The boys' eyes gleamed and Twitchy licked his lips, like a hungry dog.

"Well you won't be needing all that, now you've almost reached Bala!" said Crooked Teeth. I felt my heart beat faster.

"That's true enough," I said, as calmly as I could. "Our uncle will feed us well when we arrive. Would you fine fellows like to take what we have left? That will save us carrying it."

"Give it here!" growled Crooked Teeth. He took my bundle and flung it at Twitchy but then he grabbed at Mary's bag. He was still gripping me but I could move more easily now.

"Let me do it," said Mary, stepping away from him. "There is a knack to this bag." She pushed her hand into the front pouch and pulled out all that was left of her food. "There, I hope you enjoy it." She even managed a little smile.

Twitchy was busy with my bundle but Crooked Teeth was still not satisfied. He dropped the food she gave him on to the ground beside him and nodded at Mary's bag again.

"There's more! I can see it, there!"

I held my breath. Mary's mam had packed the food in the front pocket and put the money underneath. Was that what he could see? I looked and realised he was pointing at the bulging back pocket where Mary had put her clogs. Mary calmly turned the bag on her shoulder so that the back became the front. I hoped that the money was so well-wrapped that it wouldn't jingle. All was well and she reached in to pull out the clogs.

"I don't think you would find these very good to eat," she said in a trembling voice. I could see that she had turned her shoulder so that the pocket with the money in was shielded from his gaze. She closed her eyes and I saw her lips moving. I thought she was going to swoon as women sometimes do but maybe she was praying.

"Well," I said. "We must be off now, and leave you to enjoy your meal."

But Crooked Teeth kept hold of me and stared at me with narrowed eyes. I could tell that he didn't trust us but I was at the end of my courage and ideas and ready to give up. Then I looked over his shoulder to where

Twitchy was cramming food into his mouth as fast as he could.

"I think you will have to be quick or there may not be much left for you!"

Crooked Teeth turned and saw what was happening. With a roar, he let go of me and threw himself on Twitchy.

We left them, fighting over our food, and ran!

Even though we were very tired we kept running until we were sure the boys had not followed us. Then, as we left the hills behind and crossed the fields, we finally reached the end of the great lake. We flopped down on the grass to rest for a moment.

"Thank you again, Bryn Parry," Mary panted. "You are far wiser than me about some things. I am glad you spoke over me and kept the money safe. You were very brave."

"Huh, it was nothing," I said. "Just two skinny boys. It wasn't as though I had to fight off the Red Brigands with my bare hands!"

She looked around. "Here is the lake, but where is the town?"

A shepherd plodded past with his dogs.

"Where is the town of Bala?" Mary asked him.

"You have a few miles to walk yet, young missy," he said. "The town is at the other end of the lake and it is a very long lake."

I looked at my poor feet and groaned. Mary drooped like a flower too long out of water. We looked at the sun, which was moving down towards the far mountains.

"Do you want to rest some more?" I asked. "We could find somewhere to sleep and then reach Bala tomorrow."

"No," Mary sighed. "We are nearly there; we mustn't give up, though I had thought we would be there by now." She spoke in a small voice. "It will be dark soon and we have no lantern." I was not used to this quiet Mary.

"I will take care of you," I said, as bravely as I could. "Together we will find the way and maybe your shepherd God will help us."

Chapter Thirteen

I have never felt as tired as when we walked those last miles along the lake to Bala. My legs ached and my feet were sore. Mary plodded beside me, hardly speaking at all. The sun slipped slowly behind the mountains and we saw flocks of birds flying over the lake to their roosting places. Now and then we passed a cottage and the smell of cooked food made my mouth water. At the far end of the lake a dark smudge of buildings grew slowly nearer. Bala was waiting for us in the twilight. We passed few people on the track now but we were still wary, after our experience in the afternoon.

"I swear any robber meeting us now would hear my belly growl and think we have a huge dog walking with us nearby!" I said, trying to cheer us. Mary smiled but said nothing. I could see she was very tired now and I wondered what she was thinking. Soon she would reach Bala and have her Bible at last, but what would happen then? We had no food and no money, once the Bible was paid for. At last we reached a bridge over a river and soon the town surrounded us. What a sight it was! The track turned to cobbled road that felt strange to our bare feet. There were many stone buildings with real glass in the windows. Light shone out on to the cobbles, making the rooms look cosy and inviting. Some of the houses were tall and grand and we could see rooms inside with pictures on the walls and lots of furniture.

"The town is so big!" said Mary, staring around. A carriage rumbled by and I jumped at the sound. Dogs barked and there was still a hum of life, even at the end of the day.

"I must make myself presentable before we find the Reverend Charles' house," said Mary. She led the way down to the lakeside and there she put down her bag and took off the sling.

"My hand feels better now," she said.

I watched as she washed her face and feet, tidied her hair and smoothed down her apron. I was amazed at all this effort when the most important thing in my mind was where to find food.

Next Mary asked the way to the Reverend Charles' house and, after still more walking, we arrived at the High Street. A grand house it was, with a fine front door. A gentleman's house and not what we were used to. I hung back.

"I will wait here," I said, and I sat down under a tree while she walked up to the front door and knocked. She looked very small, standing there waiting, and I hoped whoever came to answer would be kind to her.

The door was opened by a woman who looked like a servant. Light shone out into the street. I could not hear what was said but I saw the servant take Mary inside and close the door again. Then I saw Mary pass across a lighted window in a room next to the front door. She stood as if she was waiting and I got up and crept closer to watch what happened. I looked into the room where she stood and saw a gentleman come in. He was dressed like Mr Ellis the schoolmaster but he looked older. He spoke to Mary and then she seemed to be speaking to him. I could see him listening and nodding but then he held up his hands and shook his head. Mary's shoulders drooped and then she reached into her apron pocket and pulled out her handkerchief to wipe her eyes. This did not look good! I crept closer still, until my fingers were gripping the windowsill, but I couldn't hear anything.

What had happened? Why was Mary crying? What had that man said to upset her? It had been a very long day; my legs were aching and I was so empty I feared I might blow away in a gust of wind. I didn't feel as though I could do any more protecting that day but I saw that Mary needed my help once more. I closed my eyes and tried to gather one last shred of strength. When I opened them again the room was empty!

I stepped back from the window and looked up at the house. By now it was getting really dark and I was very anxious. Where had Mary gone, and what should I do now? I made up my mind to knock at the door and demand to know what had happened to Mary, but as I stepped forward, the door opened again and out she came. The gentleman stood behind her, watching. Mary still held her handkerchief and dabbed at her eyes. Seeing her like that was all it took for me to leap into action. I pushed past her and on to the doorstep, facing the gentleman who had made her cry.

"What have you done to my friend?" I shouted. "She has worked and saved for years and years to buy her Bible. We have walked all day from far away in the mountains. We were wet to our skin and now our feet are sore. We have braved many dangers on the road; she has hurt her hand and some robbers nearly stole the money. How dare you make her cry!" The man looked startled but then he smiled and that made me even more angry. Did he think this was some kind of joke? "We walked here today because the great Reverend Thomas Charles told my friend to come here for a Bible! He said she would get one! If you don't believe me you should go and ask him yourself! I, Bryn son of Madoc Parry the shepherd, am sure he is a truthful man and he would never lie! You ask him and he will agree with me that this is no laughing matter!" I stopped for breath and realised that Mary was standing beside me, shaking my arm.

"What?" I said angrily.

"That is the Reverend Thomas Charles!" she whispered.

My mouth dropped open and I stood and stared. Was this ordinary-looking man the famous Reverend Thomas Charles? My first thought was that he didn't look very great at all. My next thought was that, if he was the great man and I had just shouted at him so angrily, I had probably ruined Mary's chances of ever getting a Bible now. I looked at Mary and then back to the man in the doorway, and then I hung my head and wished that the wind would blow me away for ever!

I felt a hand on my shoulder and a gentle voice, with a smile in it, spoke.

"All is well, Bryn Parry. Your friend will explain what has happened."

When I looked up he had gone and Mary was pulling me through the door.

"Come," she said. "The servant is to give us food, though I would not be surprised, after all that shouting, if they made you eat yours out here on the doorstep!"

I followed her back to the door. Oh my, what a house! Inside it had clean wooden floors that felt smooth and warm to my tired feet. They were covered with colourful rugs and so much furniture! We don't even have enough stools for everyone in our family to sit together and here were chairs with backs and even some soft cushions. I followed Mary, and the wonderful smell, down a passage to the kitchen where there was a feast spread out on the table. There was a pie, fresh bread and cheese and plenty to drink. The servant made me wash my hands and then she went about her work at the other end of the kitchen, leaving Mary and me to eat.

I put my head down and didn't lift it till all the plates were empty. Mary ate, too, but she did more talking and I don't think she noticed what she was eating.

"So," I said, through a big mouthful of pie. "Where's the Bible then?"

"It is quite simple, Bryn Parry," she said. "I have no Bible because they have not arrived yet from London."

I nodded as I chewed, to show I understood her.

"The Reverend Charles greeted me so kindly," she went on. "He remembered me as 'the little weaver'," she smiled at the name. "When I heard that there were no Bibles I was so disappointed. I started to cry because of being tired and having nowhere to stay and it being nearly night. The Reverend Charles was very kind and he has said that I can stay here until the Bibles arrive, which will be any day now, he's sure."

I was glad for Mary, though I wondered what my family would think. Of course I had decided to stay in Bala until Mary got her Bible, for I must make sure she got home again safely. But if I stayed away from home too long, would Mam find out that I was not at the hafod with Tada?

"That is good news," I said. "But I hope those Bibles come soon... "

* * *

*M*ary stayed two nights with the Reverend Charles' servant Catrin, in her house at the foot of the garden. I found a bed nearby, in the stables where Reverend Charles' white horse lived. I was very comfortable in my soft bed in the hayloft. In the daytime Mary helped Catrin with work about the house. Her hand didn't seem to trouble her now. The man who owned the stables let me work with the horses and paid me well with food. I think that if I am not a shepherd with Tada, I would like to work in a stable. Horses are not stupid like sheep and they smell much better.

Early on the second morning there was great excitement when the carrier brought a big box to the Reverend Charles' door. The men in the stable were talking about it so I knew that the Bibles had arrived, even before Mary came running to find me.

"Bryn Parry, it's time to go!" she called. She was hugging something close to her chest and her bag hung from her shoulders. It seemed to be very full.

"It must be a mighty big book, this Bible of yours," I said, looking at her bag.

"No," she said, smiling as she showed me the book she was holding. "It is not so very big."

She looked at my puzzled face and then laughed. "My bag is so full because Catrin has given me some fresh food for the journey home. I also have something else... "

She reached into her bag and brought out two more books. "The Reverend Charles has let me have three Bibles, instead of just the one!"

This was surprising and I had a worrying thought. "But you only had money for one Bible," I said. "How many more years will it take to pay for another two?"

"That is the wonderful thing," she replied. "The Reverend Charles said that I had paid enough already. He said he was sure that the Bibles would go to people who would love them and use them wisely and that was what was most important."

I held one of the Bibles in my hands that morning. It was the first time I had ever held a book. Its pages were clean and white and had a good smell. The writing was small and black but I could make out some letters that I knew. I was surprised that it was much smaller than the one in the church that our Reverend reads from.

"So, all those stories you tell us are in here?" I asked as I handed it back to her. Mary nodded.

"There are stories and so much more. In this book God is speaking to us and telling us of his love and his plans for us." She hugged the Bible to her. "And now I have a Bible of my own and two to share with others, so that we can hear God speak to us at any time." She looked up at the sky. "Hurry! The sun has been up for hours; we must start back at once!"

Gently she put the Bibles back into her bag and then she started to run down the street. I followed her towards the lake and the track that led us back into the mountains.

Chapter Fourteen

When Mary returned to our village with the Bibles she was greeted with excitement by many people. Even those who still thought the Society members were people to be wary of admitted that what Mary had done was a brave and marvellous thing. All of us were proud of the fact that we had three Bibles in our village, as well as the one in the church of course. As for me, well, I escaped any awkward questions and the trouble I had expected, and I told no one where I had been. Mary and I can speak of it and it will be our secret until I am old enough and big enough to tell it and not get a beating from Tada!

The Bibles are all being put to good use and many of us children, and some grown-ups, are now learning to read from one or other of them. Mary still reads to us when we have time from our work and we are learning about the shepherd God and what he is like.

It is strange that one book can hold such power but I can see that the people in our village are changing. There is not so much fear and talk of Them on the Mountain these days. There are still some though, like Tada, who say all this Bible reading is as much moonshine as the Reverend's bleating on a Sunday. They still say that we need to remember the power of men like Mr Rhys. Others look shocked when they hear people mock the power of Them. They make the sign against evil, just in case.

That is why I decided to do this. That is why I am up here, with the sun at my back and the wind buffeting me.

"It's all nonsense!" I told them. "I'll prove it to you. I will stay on the Mountain all night and in the morning you will see who is right!"

Brave words, and I began to regret them when I climbed up here yesterday, as the sun went down. Even though climbing the Mountain is something I have always wanted to do it is not easy to come up here alone. When you leave the last stream behind there is no sound but the wind and the "Kronk-kronk" of the ravens. Mam and Tada could not stop me, now that I am grown and doing a man's work. But I began to wish I had let them persuade me not to go. It is a bleak and lonely place, up here on the summit. There is more rock than grass and little shelter. I wrapped myself in a blanket and curled into a cranny of rock to watch the sunset. The sky flamed as though the mountains were on fire and then the light faded and the stars came out.

Rocks can make fearsome shapes against a darkening sky and it took all my courage not to run from what I imagined I could see. All my life I have heard the frightening stories about the Mountain. Although it was easy to laugh at them down in the valley, up here in the dark it was a battle, I can tell you! To keep my mind from telling me lies I thought of the long walk to Bala. We had faced dangers; real ones and ones in our minds. We had been kept safe, all the way there and back. I remembered how, when I was full of fear, Mary and I had shouted the shepherd psalm as we crept along the path in the mist. All last night I repeated it, hoping that the shepherd God would hear me and lead me safe through the valley of the shadow of Death. I thought of Mary. She believes that what she has learned about God is true and didn't give up when others were unkind. She saved her pennies for many years and then walked to an unknown place because what she believed in was so important. Well, if Mary could do it, so could I!

So, here I am; alive and unharmed. What do you think of that? Ha! I do not fear you now, Giant Idris. Not you or the great ghostly hounds of Gwyn the Hunter. I have sat up here on your mountain throne all night and now I know you have no power over me. I am learning about a Greater One, who made your mountain and all that I can see from here. I am learning that his power is stronger than anything and his love is so great that there is no room left for fear of you!

More Lifepath Adventures

A Land of Broken Vows
Steve Dixon

It's 1141, and murder and death are sweeping over England. Knights, Barons and Kings make and break promises in order to get power and money. At the monastry of St Mary in the Wilds, John, the son of a Knight, seems shut away from all the broken promises, but soon even the monks can't resist the temptation to break their vows to God. John is plunged into a world of danger and lies – will he be able to proect his friend?

£4.99   978 184427 371 3

Hard Rock
Fay Sampson

Collan can't wait to join his dad and brother as a Hard Rock man – a miner – but it doesn't take long for him to realise that the mine is a dangerous place. How will he cope having to work with his father's drunk workmate? And what difference will the visit of John Wesley make?

£4.99   978 184427 372 0

Pilgrim
Eleanor Watkins

Tom was all alone – what was he going to do? Then he remembered something his mother said. She said that if anything were to happen to her, he should go back to her home village of Scrooby, where good people, people called Separatists, would look after him. Should he join the Separatists – the Pilgrim Fathers – on their journey to the new world?

£4.99   978 184427 373 7

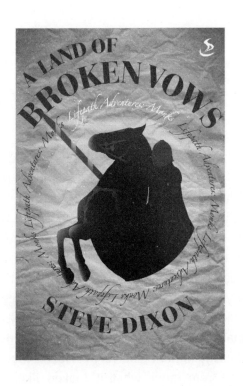

A Land of Broken Vows

Want a sneak preview of another *Lifepath Adventure*?
Read on for the first chapter of *A Land of Broken Vows*...

Chapter One

The forest fight

My father promised he would never leave me. That promise is one of the first things I remember. I must have been about 4 years old at the time. I was sitting on his knee by the open fire in the big room of our Hall. I can remember the heat of the fire making my cheeks burn. And I can remember the orange light on the rushes that were spread across the flagstone floor. I'd just asked my father why I didn't have a mother like the village children had and like Siward the boy who served our food. I had a nursemaid, Arlette, but I knew she wasn't my mother. I remember my father being very close, his face very big, but I can't remember what it looked like. All I can remember is the heat and the warm, flickering light. I can't even remember the first things he said; just that somehow he told me my mother had died when I was being born. It's something that happens quite often, I learned as I grew up. I soon found out I wasn't the only motherless child in the world. I think I must have asked my father if he was going to die and leave me, because he held me tight and said, "John, I will never leave you. That's a promise."

I remember those words exactly. And I remember I didn't know what a promise was, but it sounded a strong word the way my father said it. Something about the way my father held me tight, and the warmth and the light made me feel that everything would be all right. Whenever I felt sad or upset in years to come, those words and that scene would rush into my mind to calm me and give me courage. I think I must have been about 5 when I asked Arlette what a promise was. She told me it was something someone said they were going to do.

"And do they do it?" I asked.

"That depends if they're a person who keeps their promises," she told me.

I can remember a few more details about this conversation. We were in a little room at the end of the Hall. There was a tapestry hanging against the stone of one of the walls. It showed riders with spears hunting a stag. I always loved to look at it – at all the details, the tiny forest creatures and the beautiful stag. It was daytime when I asked about promises. It feels like a morning scene in my memory. The sun was bright through the little, high up window. Arlette had been teaching me my letters and I was making my first words. French words, of course – that was all we spoke in the Hall. I could speak English with the Saxon children from the village, but I don't think they write their language down.

"Is my father a person who keeps his promises?" I asked.

She came and held my face between both her hands.

"Your father is a knight," she said. "Knights must always keep their promises."

* * *

It was seven years since my father made me his promise, and six years since I learned what a promise was. And now my father lay bleeding on the ground, his head in my lap, his breath coming in groaning gasps like someone deep asleep. His eyes were open though. They were staring up into the forest branches that roofed us in, but they looked unfocused, unseeing. I was sure he was dying. Two other men lay dead beside the forest path we had been travelling on. Three knights' horses and my pony shifted about amongst the trees, waiting for someone to take charge of them.

It was supposed to be a great day out – a treat for me. My father and I had been on our way to Baron Gilbert's castle. He was our lord and my father had to serve him in return for the land we had. Every so often Father and all the other knights who owed Baron Gilbert service were called to the castle to a court where they would discuss the affairs of the Baron's estates and settle disputes. Father held a little court in the Moot Hall in our village to sort out affairs in his manor. For the last year or so, he'd let me stand beside his chair so that I could see how things were decided. He'd explained to me that this was how the whole country of England was run – little courts in little halls, and bigger courts in castles, right up to the King, meeting with his great barons. This was how the law and the peace were kept. Or had been in the time of old King Henry – "The Lion of Justice" as they called him. But this was the year of our Lord Jesus 1141, the old king had been dead six years, no one seemed to be sure who was king any more, and my father lay dying in my arms.

I wasn't crying. I must have been in shock. I didn't know what to do. My heart was thumping and my hands felt clumsy. I kept stroking my father's hair as if that would do some good. It was what Arlette did to me when I was ill. He hadn't had his war helmet on when we'd been attacked. It was a warm April day and he hadn't even been wearing his mail coat. We'd been riding happily through the forest pointing out the birds and the squirrels to each other, looking forward to the feast and the entertainment there would be after the court business, when suddenly my father had stopped his horse and listened. Then he'd shouted to me, "Ride on – gallop!" and he'd turned his horse and whisked his sword from its scabbard.

I did as he told me, but a moment later I heard a yell and I pulled my pony up. Swinging round I saw two knights, helmeted and with shield and lance in hand charging towards my father. I was 11 years old and had no weapon. I could do nothing to help and my father had been right to tell me to run. But how can a son run away when his father is about to be killed? I sat on my pony, gripping the reigns and stared. Then, for a moment, I thought perhaps my father wouldn't die. The forest path was narrow and his attackers could only come at him in single file. He had no time to unsling the shield that was hanging across his shoulders but he swung his sword, knocking aside the first man's lance and as the knight rode past my father somehow managed to catch him a blow in the back of the neck, just below his helmet.

He crashed off his horse, hit a tree trunk, fell to the ground and lay still. But the second knight charged in straight behind the first and my father had no time to parry his lance. It caught him in the ribs and sent him, too, tumbling to the forest floor. I shouted out, and maybe that was what gave my father his chance. The knight saw me and charged on down the path in my direction. I should have turned and fled, but I couldn't move. My father had begun to teach me the use of the sword, but even if I'd had one, I would have had no chance against the charge of a grown warrior. If I'd had a weapon that day, I don't think I would even have drawn it. He came so close that I could hear the panting of his horse, but then the man pulled on the reigns and dragged his horse to a halt. He paused for a moment, maybe realising for the first time that I was only a boy, and not worth his trouble. I can remember nothing of his face, just two hard, dark eyes on either side of the nose piece of his helmet. The horse snorted, and the rider swung it round, levelled his lance and charged at my father again. But by then my father had managed to get to his feet and bring his shield round to protect his body. At the last moment, before the man's lance hit his shield, my father stepped to one side. He had been standing with his back to a tree and the man drove his lance straight into it. The shock shattered the weapon and jerked him out of his saddle. He yelled in pain as he landed and before he could struggle to his feet my father was standing over him. They struck each other at the same time. The man, swiping wildly from the ground slashed my father's thigh, but my father's blow was a clean thrust into the neck. He put all his weight behind it and the man's chain mail gave way. He died instantly.

I trotted back to the scene and jumped from my pony, but my relief only lasted a moment. The sword slipped from my father's hand and he tottered towards me as if he were drunk. He was a few paces away when he dropped to his knees and knelt, swaying, with his arms wrapped round his chest. Blood was running down his leg and I could see that it was also oozing out from under the hand he had pressed to his ribs. He looked at me and I think he tried to smile, then he toppled forward. I got down beside him and heaved until I was able to roll him over. His face looked white and as I stroked his hair he started to shake.

I took his head between my hands and turned it so that his glazed eyes were pointing at me then I bent my face down to his and shouted, "Father! Don't leave me! You said you wouldn't! You said you'd never leave me! You promised!" I kept on shouting, "You promised!" over and over, but I was sure it was hopeless. And then something happened to his eyes. They seemed to focus again and I knew that he could see me. He groaned and lifted his hand to hold on to my arm. I stopped shouting and began to cry.

He took three or four gasping breaths, then managed to speak.

"Sit me up, John," he whispered.

I got behind him and managed to lever his shoulders off the ground. I kept on pushing until he was sitting. He lolled forward and it was several moments, before he spoke again – a croak that I could only just hear.

"Fetch horse," he said. "Can't walk."

I knew my father's horse well and it came easily to my voice. It stood steadily as my father draped his arms across its back.

"Kneel down - make a back, son," he said. "Have to stand on you."

I did as he told me and my father used me as a mounting block. He groaned and growled as he hauled himself onto the horse's back, but at last he was on, with his head lying on the creature's neck and his arms clasped tight around it.

"Sword and shield," he mumbled.

I fetched them and managed to secure them to my pony's back.

"Lead horse," my father instructed.

"Home?" I asked.

"No - onward," he told me.

So I took the stallion's bridle and led him along the path, away from the scene of the ambush. My pony followed on without trouble. But the knights' horses stayed with their fallen masters.

I'd been to Baron Gilbert's castle before and I knew it was still a long way off. At a normal pace it would take some hours, but creeping along as we were I was sure we wouldn't arrive before nightfall. My father groaned at the slightest jolt and soon he began muttering like a man in a fever. I couldn't see how he would survive. But then the path crossed a stream. I stopped and brought water in my cupped hands. My father managed to suck some of it up and I splashed the rest on his face. Then he made a great effort to speak.

"Path," he croaked, "down."

The pathway to the castle continued across the stream, but I could see there was another, narrower track leading down an incline, following the course of the water.

"Go down," my father repeated.

So I led his horse carefully down the track and my pony followed. Every now and then I would stop for more water, but my father was no longer able to drink so I just used the water to cool him. He was rambling deliriously and I knew I would get no further directions from him. The situation seemed hopeless. There was nothing for it but to keep on following the track and see where it led.

* * *

It led into a valley, and before we got to the bottom, the trees gave way to open hillside. The forest had been cleared and the slopes were dotted with sheep, scores of them. On the common ground at our village we grazed cattle, and everyone kept pigs, but no one had sheep. I stood still for a moment and listened to the occasional baa sound they made. I shut my eyes, exhausted. The sound of the sheep and the stream running on down the valley side lulled me and I almost went to sleep on my feet. Then a shout roused me. In the bottom of the valley, the stream joined a little river, and on the river bank a man was standing, waving his arms. He seemed to have some kind of black apron hanging down his front, but the rest of him was covered in a long, wide-sleeved robe that shone white in the afternoon sun.

I had no idea who or what he was, but he was another human being, and he had shouted in French. Perhaps he could give help. I bent close to my father's face and whispered to him, "I've found someone. It's going to be all right. Don't give up. Remember your promise."

He was still murmuring, so I knew I hadn't lost him yet, but his arms were slack around the horse's neck. I had to hold him on as we crept carefully downwards. The man in white could obviously see the difficulty. He hitched his robe up, showing bare legs above his stockings, and began to run up the slope.

"Dear God in heaven preserve you!" he said when he reached us and saw the state my father was in. "Come on – there's no time to lose."

Then he heaved his robe up still further, showing that he wore absolutely nothing underneath, and to my amazement he sprang onto the horse's back behind my father. He took the reins in one hand and passed the other arm round my father's waist, hauling his body upright. The sleeve of the man's robe fell back to show a massive forearm, bulging with muscle.

"Follow me, boy," he shouted, "and be quick about it."

Then without waiting for an answer he rode off at a smart trot, my father jiggling in front of him like a child's doll. As he rode down the hill I noticed that the top of his head was completely shaved. The only hair he had was in a neat band running all around his head like a crown.

I had to hang my father's shield on my back and lay his sword across my lap so that I could sit on my pony. I must have looked a strange warrior, dwarfed by his arms, as I trotted after the man who'd taken my father. There was a bend in the valley and the man in white had disappeared round it before I caught up. I wondered where he could be leading me. Some peasant's hovel no doubt. But at least it would be somewhere for my father to rest. If he could rest and we could bandage his wounds and he could survive his fever perhaps there was hope. But the wound to his chest was serious, and even the cut on his thigh could be fatal. I knew strong men in our village who had died from the simplest of injuries – a cut from a clumsy stroke with a scythe at corn harvest could cost a life if the wound went bad. I had small hope that a peasant too poor to afford breeches would have any medicines to deal with my father's wounds.

Then I rode round the bend and saw what was at the end of the valley. First there was a level area laid out in fields. Further on were a few buildings, then a wooden boundary wall and inside that I could see the roofs of many more buildings. One stood out above all the others. It had a tall, pitched roof, like a lord's hall, and a stout square tower like something from a castle. The man in white was racing on towards a gateway in the wall and shouting, but I was too far away to hear what he said. I saw another white-robed figure pull the gates open, then I noticed they were dotted all over the place, like seagulls in a field.

As I came close to the gate, I called out to one of the men who was clearing brambles beside the path. He stared at me, an 11-year-old boy, weighed down with a shield and a warrior's sword, with as much amazement as I was staring at him.

"What is this place?" I shouted.

In my haste, I'd spoken in French and I realised that if he was working on the land he was probably Saxon, but he replied in my own language without hesitation, and in an accent more cultured than my own.

"This is the Abbey of St Mary," he told me. "St Mary in the Wilds."

Great books from Scripture Union

Fiction

Mista Rymz, Ruth Kirtley £3.99, 978 184427 163 4
Flexible Kid, Kay Kinnear £4.99, 978 184427 165 8
The Dangerous Road, Eleanor Watkins £4.99, 978 184427 302 7
Where Dolphins Race with Rainbows, Jean Cullop £4.99, 978 184427 383 5
A Captive in Rome, Kathy Lee £4.99, 978 184427 088 0
Fire By Night, Hannah MacFarlane £4.99, 978 184427 323 2
The Scarlet Cord, Hannah MacFarlane £4.99, 978 184427 370 6

The Lost Book Trilogy

The Book of Secrets, Kathy Lee £4.99, 978 184427 342 3
The Book of Good and Evil, Kathy Lee £4.99, 978 184427 368 3
The Book of Life, Kathy Lee £4.99, 978 184427 369 0

Fiction by Patricia St John

Rainbow Garden £4.99, 978 184 27 300 3
Star of Light £4.99, 978 184427 296 9
The Mystery of Pheasant Cottage £4.99, 978 184427 296 9
The Tanglewoods' Secret £4.99, 978 184427 301 0
Treasures of the Snow £5.99, 978 184427 298 3
Where the River Begins £4.99, 978 184427 299 0

Bible and Prayer

The 10 Must Know Stories, Heather Butler £3.99, 978 184427 326 3
10 Rulz, Andy Bianchi £4.99, 978 184427 053 8
Parabulz, Andy Bianchi £4.99, 978 184427 227 3
Massive Prayer Adventure, Sarah Mayers £4.99, 978 184427 211 2

God and you!

No Girls Allowed, Darren Hill and Alex Taylor £4.99, 978 184427 209 9
Friends Forever, Mary Taylor £4.99, 978 184427 210 5

Puzzle books

Bible Codecrackers: Moses, Valerie Hornsby £3.99, 978 184427 181 8
Bible Codecrackers: Jesus, Gillian Ellis £3.99, 978 184427 207 5
Bible Codecrackers: Peter & Paul, Gillian Ellis £3.99, 978 184427 208 2

Available from your local Christian bookshop or from
Scripture Union Mail Order, PO Box 5148, Milton Keynes MLO, MK2 2YX
Tel: 0845 07 06 006 Website: www.scriptureunion.org.uk/shop
All prices correct at time of going to print.